The Railroad Tycoon Rescue

Paulette D. Marshall

Paulette D. Marshall

The Railroad Tycoon Rescue

The Railroad Tycoon Rescue

Paulette D. Marshall

Praising God for these words and giving Him the glory

Marshall Mountains Publishing

Paulette D. Marshall
Copyright@2020 by Paulette D. Marshall
First Edition: August 2024.>All rights reserved.
First Edition: March 18, 2024

All rights reserved.
No portion of this book may be reproduced in any form without written permission from the author, except as permitted by U. S. copyright law.

This is a work of fiction. Names, characters, businesses, places events, locales, and incidents either are the product of the author's imagination or are used in a fictitious manner. Any resemblance to actual persons, living or dead, business establishments, or actual events is purely coincidental.

Special thanks to my **ARC/Street** team readers!

Thank you to all who read and reviewed my books.

Cover Design: JoAnn's Book Cover Design.

Editor: My wonderful editor, Sarah Lamb

The Railroad Tycoon Rescue: by Paulette D. Marshall. All Bible verses used are NIV, so they are easier to understand.

Join my newsletter https://bit.ly/3Revnq2. All my links in one convent place: https://bit.ly/3Revnq2

Marshall Mountains Publishing

The Railroad Tycoon Rescue

Author

For more about my books

Follow on BookBub: https://bit.ly/3Wuph6Z

Newsletter: https://bit.ly/3Revnq2

Join Paulette D. Marshall Reading Community:
https://bit.ly/3F1aadr

Webpage Paulette D. Marshall:
https://bit.ly/4a6prbv

Amazon https://amzn.to/3DzH56N

All of my links in one convenient place:
https://bit.ly/3C4p5S3

Marshall Mountains Publishing

Paulette D. Marshall

Table of Contents

Chapter One	7
Chapter Two	21
Chapter Three	29
Chapter Four	37
Chapter Five	49
Chapter Six	61
Chapter Seven	69
Chapter Eight	81
Chapter Nine	91
Chapter Ten	103
Chapter Eleven	113
Chapter Twelve	125
Chapter Thirteen	135
Chapter Fourteen	143
Chapter Fifteen	153
Epilogue	161
Bible Verse	168
Recipe	160
About the Author	171

The Railroad Tycoon Rescue

Chapter One

Cornelius

Cornelius Vanderbilt was a man poised to inherit a fortune if he could meet the stipulations laid out in his grandfather's will. Wealth was woven into the fabric of his family and had been for years, but it came with strings, complications, and pressures that sometimes felt suffocating.

One such complication was the marriage his grandfather had arranged for him. The woman was beautiful on the outside, but cold and calculating on the inside. It was clear that her interest lay not in Cornelius himself, but in the Vanderbilt fortune. A life bound to someone who saw him as nothing more than a bank account was a nightmare he refused to entertain.

Cornelius wanted more. He yearned for a marriage with companionship, mutual respect, and, if he dared to dream, love. He couldn't imagine finding that with the woman his grandfather had selected.

Time, however, was not on his side. According to the will, Cornelius had to be married by his twenty-third birthday to inherit his grandfather's railroad empire. Without fulfilling this condition, he would have no control over the family business, no say in the company he'd been groomed to lead. And the deadline was fast approaching.

Frustration gnawed at him as he reflected on how he'd ended up in this predicament. He wasn't short on social connections. He'd had plenty of dates and even a few relationships. But none of them felt right. None of them were with the kind of woman he could imagine building a life with.

Now, faced with an impossible timeline and the weight of his family's expectations, Cornelius found himself considering an unconventional solution: a mail-order bride. It wasn't ideal, but it might be his best chance to secure the future he wanted both for himself and for the company he loved.

Cornelius was caught off guard when he heard his grandmother's voice cut through the silence. "Cornelius, these agencies take pride in making perfect matches and building their reputation. I was speaking with Ester the other day, and she mentioned that their agency boasts a ninety-five percent success rate in pairing the right couples together. She even hinted that it could be higher. Ester claims she prays while she reads the applications. I think you could trust her. After all, she is your cousin," she said, her tone confident.

He hadn't even realized she had entered the room. It was funny how his grandmother always

The Railroad Tycoon Rescue

seemed to know exactly what was on his mind. He straightened, feeling slightly exposed. "I spoke to my lawyer this morning," he said, trying to regain his composure. "George confirmed that marrying a mail-order bride would meet the conditions of the will. As long as we are legally married, it'll satisfy the terms."

Cornelius paused, frowning at the oddness of his own words. "Legally married," he repeated almost to himself. The phrase seemed redundant. Why would his lawyer even need to clarify that? Of course, they'd be legally married. What other kind of marriage was there?

His grandmother, however, didn't seem fazed as she continued to walk slowly into the room.

"I can't believe that young lady broke her agreement, saying you don't have enough money. Who does she think she is?" Grandmother's voice was sharp with indignation.

Conelius gave a short laugh. "I, for one, am happy, Grandmother. Prissy was a cold, money-hungry woman. Beauty was only on the outside of her. All she ever cared about was the size of my bank account, not me." He shook his head, the memory of his almost fiancée fading away like a bad dream. "I've always dreamed of having the kind of relationship you and Grandfather had, built on love, trust, and respect. If I had married Prissy, I got the feeling I would've ended up sleeping in the carriage house or in the guest bedroom."

His grandmother smiled at him, her eyes softening. "You're right to want more Cornelius. Marriage should be about more than convenience or wealth. You deserve a real partnership like your grandfather, and I had. Don't settle for less."

"I won't," he promised. "That's why I'm considering the mail-order bride. At least those women are genuinely looking for companionship, not just a bank account."

Grandmother sat down gracefully, then rang the small silver bell on the table. A maid appeared promptly.

"Please, serve me my tea here," Grandmother said with her usual calm authority.

"Yes, ma'am," the maid responded, disappearing.

Turning back to Cornelius, Grandmother raised an eyebrow. "Are you truly signing up for a mail-order bride? You're going to run out of time, you know. The wills deadline is fast approaching."

Cornelius nodded. "I plan on heading over this morning to fill out the paperwork. Cousin Ester assured me we could work within my time frame. But there's one thing I need your help with."

"Oh? And what might that be?" Grandmother asked, her curiosity piqued.

"I plan on using the name Cory on the application, not my full name Cornelius. I don't want someone to marry me just for my wealth or for my family's wealth. If this works. I want to be sure she's interested in me, not my money," he explained. "I'm praying that whoever responds to my ad will at least want to build a friendship, if not more. I just need your help keeping up the charade."

Grandmother's eyes twinkled with approval. "A wise move Cornelius. I'll go along with it but be careful. Secrets, no matter how well intentioned, have a way of complicating things. I think you deserve more than just being friends. I am going to pray that whoever answers the ad will want to be a real wife."

Cornelius couldn't shake the feeling that his grandmother, as always, was right. Secrets had a way of turning even the best of intentions into tangled messes. But there was no time for second-guessing now.

"I have one last piece of advice for you, Cornelius," his grandmother said. "Luke 12:22-26. Then Jesus said to his disciples: Therefore I tell you don't worry about your life, what you will eat, or about your body, what you will wear. Life is more than food, and the body more than the clothes. Consider the ravens: They do not sow or reap, they have no storeroom or barn; yet God feeds them. And how much more valuable you are than birds! Since you cannot do this very little thing, why do you worry about the rest?"

As Cornelius listened to her, he realized that God indeed had control over his life. Worrying about it all was a waste of time. Now if he could just turn it all over to God and let him deal with it and not take it back.

After finishing tea with her, Cornelius felt the weight of his looming deadline more than ever, but he knew that God was in control. He couldn't delay any longer. Time was slipping away, and he had to take action.

Rising from his chair, he walked quickly with purpose for the butler. The familiar, composed figure of Mr. Hargrove appeared promptly at the doorway.

"Have my horse ready," Cornelius instructed, his voice steady but his mind racing with the next steps of his plan.

"Yes, sir," Hargrove replied with a nod, turning to carry out the order.

Cornelius took a deep breath, glancing at his grandmother one last time before heading out. The clock was ticking, and soon enough, he'd find out if this gamble of finding a bride through the agency would lead him to the companionship and love he so desperately desired, or to an entirely new set of problems.

As he rode into town Cornelius spent the time praying.

Once there, Cornelius tied his horse to the hitching post and took a moment to steady himself before walking into the mail-order bride agency.

The Railroad Tycoon Rescue

The agency had only been here for about a year, but they had two other locations open in Chicago and New York. It had garnered a solid reputation for bringing people together. He prayed that the office wouldn't be too busy. The last thing he wanted was for anyone to recognize him or overhear his business.

As he stepped inside, the small bell above the door chimed softly, announcing his arrival. The room smelled faintly of lavender, and wooden floors creaked under his boots. To his relief, the place wasn't crowded, just a quiet, tidy space with a desk toward the back where Ester typically handled the applications.

Ester and her brother had opened this location just after Ester was married. It didn't hurt that she had been a mail-order bride herself, understanding firsthand the delicate nature of these arrangements. What she didn't suspect was to have cousins that lived nearby.

"Good morning, cousin," Ester greeted him with a warm smile as she looked up from her ledger.

"Good morning, Ester," Cornelius replied.

Ester asked, "How may I help you?"

"I have a delicate situation, and I am in need of a mail-order bride before my twenty third birthday which you know is quickly approaching."

Ester looked at him, "I do know, and I was curious about how that was going, but I didn't want to ask."

"It's not going so well. That's where you come in," Cornelius replied.

"Please have a seat and let's get all the information down and see what we can do," Ester suggested.

"This will stay between us?" Cornelius asked a little concerned.

"Yes, of course. You can rest assured that everything is confidential. What we discuss here will stay here between us."

Taking a deep breath, Cornelius continued. "I have less than three months to marry, or I lose my inheritance, as you know. It's a stipulation in Grandfather's will. I hadn't planned to rush into anything, but circumstances have forced my hand. I need a bride, and fast."

Ester nodded, her pen poised over the ledger. "You're not the first to find themselves in such a situation. Luckily, as you know, we specialize in swift matches without sacrificing quality. I for one am glad you didn't marry what's her name."

Cornelius smiled. He knew Ester knew the woman's name, and he was glad she didn't mention it. He had known several of his family members didn't like her.

The Railroad Tycoon Rescue

"Now, let's start with what you're looking for in a wife," Ester said, ready to write things down.

Cornelius hesitated, feeling awkward about what to say. He hadn't exactly given much thought to the specific qualities he wanted in a wife. He had always imagined it would happen naturally, as it had with his grandparents. But now the time was ticking.

"I suppose I'm looking for someone who's kind, trustworthy, and .... grounded. I don't care much about appearance, just someone with a good heart and someone who understands the importance of family. Please, no one flighty or money hungry."

Ester scribbled his words down, nodding as she wrote. She agreed with him that family was important. Ester was eager to make sure she found the right wife for him.

"There is one thing. though. I would like to use a different name on the application to avoid any…unwanted attention," Cornelius hesitantly stated.

"Understood," Ester said, looking up at him with reassurance. Her husband had used a different name in his letters when they corresponded, so the request wasn't that unusual. She knew the trouble Cornelius already had, and had experienced a little of it herself. "I'll make sure the application reflects that. We'll move quickly, but we won't rush to the wrong match. Our priority is to find someone who fits your needs and shares your values. I make sure to thoroughly check all our applications."

Cornelius relaxed slightly, feeling more confident in his decision.

"I have letters here that you can read. I believe there might be a couple suitable matches in this stack," Ester said, as she quickly picked out a few letters. "We might get lucky and you can find someone you want to write back to."

Cornelius felt a little scared and unsure. "I'm not sure what I would write."

"My suggestion is that you write a letter just like you're talking to her. This is your chance to get to know each other better and ask questions," Ester explained. "There is no commitment yet. Just relax and be yourself."

Before Cornelius could answer, Malcom entered the room and said, "Good morning, darling." Once he noticed him, he said, "Good morning, Cornelius. Sorry, I didn't see you sitting there. I guess I only have eyes for my beautiful wife."

A little nervous that Malcom might know what he was doing there Cornelius said, "Good morning, Malcom."

"Cornelius, there is nothing wrong with getting help. I sent off for a mail-order bride myself," Malcom admitted as he looked at his wife with a smile. "If you want any suggestions from a male point of view, just let me know. Your secret is safe with me."

Ester handed Cornelius three letters to look at. "Read through these letters, and tell me if you see one that interests you."

Cornelius read the first letter and set it back down saying, "No thank you." He started reading the second letter. Setting it down with the first letter he shook his head no. Picking up the last he read it. Finding the letter intriguing, he decided to reread it again. "There is something about this letter and yet I'm just not sure."

"Would you like to write back to her?" Ester asked. She was hoping they could find him someone quickly, since it would take time for the bride to travel.

Cornelius paused for a moment, considering his options.

"I think," Ester said, breaking the silence, "since you haven't found a letter that really speaks to you, it might be best if you write an ad yourself. Just describe what you're looking for."

She handed him a sheet of paper. "While you're doing that, I'll prepare the rest of my paperwork. Even though you are family, I think a contract would be the best. It will protect you and your mail-order bride. Just in case something should happen or someone should look into it. What name would you like on your contract?"

"Cory," Cornelius replied. "It is a name that I am most comfortable with."

Ester handed Cornelius a piece of paper and a quill. The inkpot was already sitting on the table so he could write his ad.

"I'm a twenty-two-year-old man seeking a woman who can read and write. Someone to share quiet evenings with after a long day's work. She should know how to manage a household and, most importantly, be a woman of faith."

Cornelius showed Ester what he had written down.

Ester smiled at him, "That looks perfect to start out with."

"I thought about adding that she should be able to entertain guests occasionally," Cornelius admitted. "But I figured that might give away the fact that I have money. I don't want someone to marry me just for the money."

"It might if you added that. Since we have a similar background, I understand what you're saying," Ester agreed, "but I will keep that in mind and set aside letters from young ladies who would be capable of handling entertaining and your business needs."

She handed him the contract. "Here is the contract. There's a new clause in our agreements called the 'rescue clause.' It states that if one of our mail-order brides is kidnapped, taken hostage, or in dire need of help, you, along with all the other mail-order husbands, are required to band together to find her and bring her back safely."

Not thinking anything of the 'rescue clause,' Cornelius read over the contract. He checked the dollar cost for the mail-order service on the contract and the amount for the train ticket along with travel money for the bride. "I want to make sure my bride has enough money for food and essentials if she should need it."

"That is a very wise decision, and I'm personally glad to hear that. I am sure she would appreciate it too. I will add that into your contract," Ester said. "Do you want your lawyer to read it before you sign? I suggest that you have him look at it."

"I believe everything is in order. I must request that we expedite this as quickly as possible," Cornelius encouraged as he signed the paper.

Ester nodded her head in understanding. "I will do my best. This will appear in the papers tomorrow in several cities and states." She handed him a copy of his contract, which he folded and put in the pocket of his jacket.

Cornelius debated about sending his Pullman car to pick up his bride, but that would scream wealth and not a wise thing to do. He felt bad that she would have to ride on those hard chairs and all that soot. It couldn't be helped.

Finally, he said, "Thank you. I would offer her a Pullman car, but I would prefer she didn't know how rich I am, at least until after the ceremony."

"While I understand your reasoning, I hope you realize the consequences of not telling her everything before the wedding," Ester carefully warned him. She understood what he was talking about since she'd had issues with men wanting to marry her because of her family money, which they wanted.

"That is the second time someone has warned me about consequences. While I do understand what you are saying, all I can promise is that I will pray about it," Cornelius stated.

"Starting out a marriage with a lie is never good," Malcom expressed. "I had a couple of secrets that I revealed before the wedding ceremony. I suggest you consider that. Marriage can be hard enough as it is to adjust to, and now you're adding more on top of that."

Cornelius couldn't agree more with Malcom, but he was afraid that a woman would only want to marry him because of his money. After all, he was almost twenty-three years old and still single.

His grandmother had told him he just hadn't met the right woman yet and God had someone special just for him. He hoped it was true.

The Railroad Tycoon Rescue
Chapter Two

Etta

Etta had no other choice. All the eligible men in her small town had either gone to war, were old, or already married, and she wasn't willing to settle for the few that remained. Jack, the man she had been betrothed to, went off to the war and never returned. It had been months since she last heard anything from him, and the hope that once flickered in her heart had long since dimmed.

Mabel, her best friend, had already offered to take her in. "Etta, you can't keep going like this," Mabel had said with concern in her eyes, her voice soft yet insistent. Etta knew Mabel was right. She was losing weight, and despite her friends' attempts to help by slipping her bits of meat and flour, it wasn't enough. The bank would be repossessing her home, and there was no stopping it even if she wanted to. Times were tough for everyone, but Etta knew she couldn't survive much longer on her own.

Desperation seemed to hang over her like a cloud. So many were suffering after the war.

Etta's options were slim, either move in with her friend, or become a mail-order bride.

Yesterday at the mercantile, she spotted a flyer tacked to the wall, advertising the need for brides in the West. After glancing around to make sure no one was watching, she discreetly slipped the flyer into her pocket. The last thing she needed was to become the town gossip more than she already was.

After Etta's parents died, she tried to find work, but there just weren't any jobs to be had, especially for a female. She did manage to do a few sewing repairs, which helped pay for the mortgage on the house. But that little bit of money that she made was too little and not enough. The mounting debt was a constant weight on her shoulders. She wondered why her father had taken out the small mortgage when they had money but since he was gone, she couldn't ask him.

Now, back home after her trip to the mercantile, Etta pulled the flyer out of her dress pocket. It read, *"Women Wanted – Apply Below."*

There were a few brief notes from men seeking wives, followed by an address in Virginia City and the name Mrs. Corsello, Mail–Order Bride Company. Etta stared at the paper for a moment, her mind racing. This wasn't what she envisioned for her future, but with no other options, it seemed like her only way out.

The Railroad Tycoon Rescue

Etta sighed, thinking of Mabel's offer to stay with her and her husband. Though well-meaning, Etta knew it wasn't a long-term solution. The idea of becoming a burden to her friend left a bitter taste in her mouth. The flyer in her hand represented a lifeline, a last-ditch chance to escape her dire circumstances. With a heavy heart, Etta carefully folded the paper, knowing she would have to make a decision soon.

Etta had heard that the mail-order bride company was reputable, with many success stories from women in her town who had used it to find husbands. They spoke highly of Mrs. Corsello's careful matchmaking, and several of them were now living comfortably with kind, hardworking men. That thought offered Etta a sliver of hope, though her heart still felt heavy as she set the flyer down on top of her worn table.

After putting away the small amount of flour that she managed to buy into a tin on the shelf, Etta paused, surveying her humble home. The walls were bare, and the furniture was sparse. The floor was worn but still clean. A piano had once sat in the corner by the window. She used to love to sit there and play. But that was long gone, sold to bring in some money. It used to look so lovely with nice furniture that Mama had bought and she had positioned doilies all around the room. All the beautiful furniture had been sold. Looking down at her hands that were callused and rough, it was hard to believe that a few years ago she had soft hands.

Glancing around the room once more, she realized that even though everything was gone, the room was still filled with wonderful memories of her family when they were alive. No one could take those away. She would keep the treasured memories close to her heart.

A single tear slid down her cheek. "This place looks like a good wind could blow it over," she whispered to herself, wiping the tear away with the back of her hand. This house was once filled with love, joy, and laughter, but that was before the war. The war had torn many families apart, and she wasn't the only one to lose everything she held dear.

She pulled one of the last few pieces of paper she had from a drawer and grabbed a quill and ink well, which was getting low. Sitting down at the kitchen table, she folded her hands and bowed her head, lifting her voice to the only One who might be able to help her.

"Lord," she began softly, "I don't know if you still remember me. It feels like you've forgotten all about me. I can't blame you since I stopped coming to you when I didn't hear your answer or get an answer that I liked after Mama went to heaven. I know that's wrong, and I ask forgiveness. But I need your help, more than ever. I can't make it on my own anymore. You see how things are here…I've barely any food left, and I'm about to lose this house. If they could just wait a little longer before taking the house from me, I'd be ever so grateful."

Her voice wavered, and she blinked away more tears. "My stomach's been reminding me all day that I've hardly eaten, and I'm afraid I don't have much more to give it. If you could send a rabbit my way or some food, Lord, I would be grateful. I don't need much, just enough to get by."

She lifted her head, her eyes shining with quiet faith, and let out a deep breath. Gently touching the paper in front of her, she began writing her letter to Mrs. Corsello, hoping this was the answer she'd been praying for.

Once the letter was written, she folded it and put it in an envelope. Carefully tucking the envelope into her pocket, she pressed her fingers on the outside against the worn fabric to assure herself that it was truly there.

She thought briefly of the small vial of perfume she had left, for a moment wishing she could add just a drop to the envelope, but decided against it. That perfume, made years ago with her mama, was precious rose petals and lemon peel steeped together to create something light and sweet. It had been one of their special projects, along with homemade soap, and now both were almost gone.

The perfume felt too dear to waste on a letter, no matter how important it was. She'd save it for a moment that truly needed it, though she couldn't quite imagine when that might be. With a soft sigh, she smoothed the outline of the envelope again and thought of her mama, wishing she were still here to offer guidance, to tell her everything would be alright.

For now, all Etta could do was put her faith in God as she continued to pray for an answer from the mail-order bride service and that God would lead her where he wanted her to go.

Grabbing a basket, Etta decided there was no sense in waiting. She'd take the letter to the post office now and forage for herbs and greens along the way. Her mother had taught her well how to use herbs for healing and which wild plants were safe to eat. Those lessons had become a lifeline over the past few months, providing her with enough to survive, although barely.

The greens she gathered, combined with the small garden she kept and the occasional catch from her snares, or fish at the lake, had managed to keep some food on the table. She'd made countless stews and soups, watering them down just enough to stretch each meal a little further.

As she stepped out of the house, the wind tugged at her worn shawl and Etta sighed. Winter wasn't too far around the corner, and she knew it would only get harder to survive. But for now, she would focus on the task at hand- delivering her letter and seeing what nature had to offer. She would also check her snares, hoping for a bit of meat to add to her stew pot tonight.

The Railroad Tycoon Rescue

With a determined breath, she started down the familiar path to town, praying quietly as she went. "Lord, I could sure use a blessing today."

The walk to the post office was a good distance, but Etta didn't mind. Along the way, she found a few wild greens and herbs to add to her dinner.

Her spirits lifted when she checked her snare and saw a plump rabbit caught in it. Maybe tonight she could make a heartier stew, and if she was careful with the little flour she had, she could even whip up some dumplings. It wouldn't be a feast, but it would fill her belly and give her some comfort on another lonely night.

Once at the post office, Etta handed over the letter. As she watched the postmaster place it in the outgoing pile, a mix of hope and anxiety churned inside her. The letter was sent.

On her way home, Etta took a different route, keeping any eye out for more herbs and greens. She foraged carefully, as her mother had taught her, always leaving some behind for others or for future growth.

The sun was starting to dip below the horizon, casting a soft golden light over the landscape, and despite her worries, Etta felt a quiet sense of peace.

She clutched her basket a little tighter, a little uncertain of what the future would hold, even if tonight she had enough for a warm meal.

That was something to be thankful for. God was faithful and took care of all of her needs. She just needed to depend on him and not worry about the future.

Chapter Three

The Letters

"I am glad you stopped in today, Cornelius. I have received several letters for you to look over. There were a few that didn't suit you, so I have removed them and will match them up to a husband later. Here is your stack. I picked out the best five and set them on the top," Ester said with a smile. She was very pleased with the response.

"These are all in response to my ad?" Cornelius asked.

"Yes, I am sure we will receive more letters since it has only been a week, but you can start reading these. Maybe you will find one of them to write back. I guess I should call you Cory now, so that I don't mess up in front of your bride," Ester said.

"I haven't made a decision about that yet," Cory said. "But you are welcome to call me Cory, since most of my friends do."

"Thank you. I will," she said with a smile. "Oh, that reminds me. Malcom wanted me to invite you over for dinner on Saturday."

"I would love to come to dinner. I have been wanting to ride out and check out his new Morgan horse," Cory said.

"Malcom is proud of his new horse. He has plans to breed her with his other Morgan, I believe," Ester voiced as she moved papers around her desk.

"Morgans are a sound business investment. Especially since Morgans are sought after and they can sell for far more than you invest in them," Cory advised.

"Good to know," Ester replied. She was sure Malcom knew all about that since he was a very astute businessman.

Cory read the five letters, but he wasn't sure which one to write back. Surely you couldn't write more than one. He hesitated on what to do next.

"Can I read one more letter?" Cornelius inquired. Why did everything have to be so difficult? All Cornelius wanted was a bride, without the whole world knowing he had to resort to a mail-order agency. He supposed there was no way around it. If they couldn't have a real marriage and love each other, he was praying that they would at least become friends.

He may have money, but he learned early on that money couldn't buy everything. Despite his family's wealth, he still had chores and lessons like everyone else. Money couldn't even save his parents.

"You're welcome to read as many of those as you would like. I would appreciate it if you would return the letters that you don't think will work. I can always find them a husband," Ester assured him.

Setting one of the letters that he had read off to the side, he picked up another letter to read.

"Remember, even if you write back to one of the letters, you are not committed to marry her. This is your chance to get to know her more and her chance to get to know you. I can give you a couple more letters to read, if you would like?" Ester offered.

Cornelius read through two more letters, then paused, eyeing the one that had left him uncertain.

Yet, something about it drew him in. "I think I'll write back to this young lady." Just holding her letter made his heart speed up. The letter held a quality about it that spoke to his heart.

Ester looked at the name on the outside of the letter. This was one of the original ones she had on top for him. "I think that's an excellent choice. I am happy that you picked out the first of the five letters that I set aside for you," Ester said with a smile. She was sure that one was the best of the letters he had received so far. "All of our clients have been carefully vetted. Why don't you go ahead and write her a letter now, and I'll take care of mailing it for you."

Cory was a little scared. He wasn't sure what he should write.

Ester could tell by the look on his face that he didn't know what to do. "Write like she is sitting next to you. She is a new friend just waiting for you," Ester encouraged him as she handed him a piece of paper and a quill.

Dear Etta,

When I opened and read your letter it was like a breath of fresh air.

I am hoping we can learn a little more about each other.

I am glad to hear that you enjoy reading. I am sorry to hear that your father's book collection has been sold off. I do have a small variety of books to read, although I don't have as much time for reading as I would like. One of my favorite books to read beside the Bible is a book of poetry. What was your favorite book?

In answer to your question, yes, I attended church every Sunday. I don't live too far from town. It makes for a pleasant drive on Sundays.

I hope to hear back from you soon.

Sincerely, Cory.

"I will get this in the mail today," Ester offered.

"I can drop it off on my way out of town," Cory stated. He wanted to make sure it went out today.

Ester said, "Cory, you can ask for a picture in your next letter. That way, you will at least know what she looks like, or you can add it to this letter."

"That's a good idea. I will add it to this letter. I believe I have a picture I can add. I brought one just in case," Cory admitted. He opened the letter and added his picture to it and a note.

Here is a picture of myself. Could you please send a picture of yourself?

Thank goodness he didn't seal the letter the first time. "I will see you in a couple of weeks," Cory said.

"If I have anything for you, I will bring it to you. I know you're very busy with your railroad company. See you on Saturday," Ester said.

"See you on Saturday," Cory agreed before he left. It didn't take too long to walk to the post office and drop his letter off. He walked back to the agency and gathered the reins of his horse off the hitching post. "Come on, Sebastian. Let's get home," he said to his horse. Cory was filled with hope that this woman Etta just might be the woman for him. "Please, Lord, help me find a wife. One that will be not only my friend, but a real wife and family someday soon," Cory whispered as he rode home.

Once home, he walked into the house. As he passed the front room, Grandmother was sitting drinking tea. When she saw him, she said, "Cornelius, I am glad you're finally home. Please come have tea with me."

"Good afternoon, Grandmother. I can only stay for a few minutes since I have work that needs to be done. I did receive a letter from a young lady, and it looked promising. I decided to correspond with her and I mailed it off before I left town. Would you like to read the letter?"

"If I am not imposing, I would love to read it," Grandmother answered eagerly. She had been praying for her grandson. She wanted him to have a wife that would love him. "Would you like a cup of tea?"

Handing over the letter, he replied, "No, thank you. I would prefer a cup of lemonade. I will ring for some while you read the letter." He rang the bell for the maid.

After Grandmother read it, she said, "She sounds like a nice young lady although there isn't much to go on. I do hope she is educated and can entertain, but the most important thing is that you both get along and fall in love."

Cornelius answered, "That might be wishful thinking, but I would settle for getting along and being friends."

"I see you are using the name Cory. I guess I will have to start calling you that instead of

Cornelius, although that does pain me some since you are named after your father," Grandmother said.

Cory responded, "I know, Grandmother. and I'm sorry. I thought this might be the safest way for now. I am still praying about revealing my secret before the marriage, but will I ever be sure she isn't marrying me for my money?"

The butler came in with lemonade and handed it to Cory. He took a long drink. The lemonade hit the spot.

"You may never know the true answer to that question. I'm sorry. With family wealth comes its own set of troubles," Grandmother stated. "But you will survive. Now run along and I will see you for dinner."

Cory stood up and kissed his grandmother on the cheek, "Thank you, Grandmother. I will be in my office." His grandmother handed back the letter and smiled at him.

Cory walked to his office where there was a pile of paperwork waiting. He couldn't run the business by himself, at least not yet, but he would still do the best that he could do and hope that his adviser approved of the job he was doing.

Paulette D. Marshall

The Railroad Tycoon Rescue

Chapter Four

Possibility Of a Future

Etta worked hard around the house and outside, trying to distract herself from the mail-order bride letter she had written. It had only been a couple of weeks, but it felt much longer. The waiting was unbearable. She kept teetering between wondering if she had made the right decision and anxiously asking herself where the response to the letter was. Did he not like her? What would happen if he didn't write her back? All these questions swirled in her mind, especially when she lay in bed at night, struggling to sleep.

She had read a couple of penny novels and wondered if the West was really like that. Did they have train and stagecoach robberies? Were the men that rough and rugged? Etta figured most of it was fabricated and wasn't true. Just merely a story. Of course, her parents didn't know she had read them, but that was a long time ago. She hadn't had money for frivolous things in a long time.

The next morning, Etta walked to the mercantile to see if she had any mail, carrying her basket with her so she could forage as she walked. That morning, she had gathered three eggs. That was enough for an egg for breakfast, and she could save the others for tomorrow. Today was turning out to be a wonderful day.

Stepping into the mercantile Etta asked, "Any mail for me today, Mr. Gilman?"

Expecting to hear no, she was shocked to hear him say, "Yes, you have two letters." He handed her two envelopes.

"Thank you, Mr. Gilman," she said with a smile as she tucked them into her pocket to read later. How exciting that she had two letters.

Etta was in such a hurry to get home and read the letters that she didn't see the squirrel hole, until she felt her foot sink and pain radiated through her ankle and foot. Gently pulling her foot out of the hole, she tried to put pressure on it, but it was too painful. "I know better than not paying attention to where I am walking," she mumbled as she sat down in the dirt. Checking over her ankle without removing her boot was difficult, but she needed to keep her boot on. She didn't feel anything broken. There was a branch close by that would make a perfect walking stick.

Etta managed to get up without putting too much pressure on her hurt ankle and hobble over to the branch that was on the ground. Taking her knife out of the basket she removed the dead leaves off the branch, along with some of the smaller branches too. The end was sharp, so she wrapped a cloth that she had in her basket around it. She could work on that later if she needed to use it longer. She still had one of her father's walking canes at home that she refused to sell. Etta held the end that she wrapped and tried walking a few steps with the stick. It needed to be a little shorter, but it would work nicely until she could get home.

As she walked, she thanked God that her ankle wasn't broken. A Bible verse came to mind, "Consider it all joy, my brothers, when you meet trials of various kinds, for you know that the testing of your faith produces steadfastness. And let steadfastness have its full effect, that you may be perfect and complete, lacking in nothing," Etta recited as she slowly walked. "Lord, thank you for these trials and that you will lead me out of them in better condition than before the trails."

Walking a slower pace gave her time to take in her surroundings and spend a quiet moment with Jesus. As she foraged along the way, she realized she might have missed some of the plants had she kept her usual hurried pace. Bending down, she picked some flowers. That should brighten up the house.

As she slowly got closer to home, Etta mentally went through her herbs, considering which treatment would be best for a sprained ankle. But her thoughts kept drifting back to the letters in her pocket. If it weren't for her need to get home and tend to her ankle, she might have sat under a big tree to read them. Yet, with the swelling setting in, she knew she couldn't risk it.

Slowly she walked up the steps to her house. Once inside, she set her basket on the kitchen table and set the flowers in a cup of water. Gathering everything she would need to treat her sprained ankle took longer as she hobbled around. Her arm was starting to hurt, and her leg was throbbing. She grabbed a bowl and cloth.

Pouring just enough castor oil over the cloth to dampen it, she reached for a homemade bottle of tincture and poured out a few drops onto the damp cloth. Gathering the bottle with dried lavender, she then sprinkled a little on the cloth. Next, she picked up a ginger root and grated a little bit on the cloth.

Filling a glass with water, she took it to the rocking chair. Next, she took the bowl with the cloth in it over and set it on the table next to the rocking chair. Etta decided that she might as well get a piece of bread to eat since she was hungry, so she cut a slice and put it on a plate. She would have to leave all the foraged items on the table for the time being. Once she wrapped her ankle and let it rest a bit, she would take care of them.

Sitting down in the rocker, she realized how tired she was, and now everything hurt. As she removed her boot, her foot throbbed.

With her foot finally wrapped and resting on a log, Etta got out the two letters she had received.

One was from Mrs. Davis and the other was from Cory Vanderbilt.

Etta opened the letter from Mrs. Davis first.

Dear Miss Dixon,

I want to assure you that I will do my best to find you the perfect husband. We have a ninety-five percent rate of happy couples that are still married and have been for years.

If you have any questions or problems, please contact me. I have a contract for you to sign. You will be happy to know that we have a rescue clause. If any of our mail-order brides should get kidnapped and need to be rescued, that clause goes into effect. Rest assured that you will be rescued. We have only had to use this once, but it's nice to know that if something happens there is a plan in place.

Please fill out the form and return it to me.

I look forward to meeting you soon.

Sincerely, Ester Davis.

Etta appreciated the letter from Ester. She seemed kind and she appreciated that she took time to write to her. Etta slipped the letter back in the envelope.

Pulling the next letter out of the envelope, she took a moment to breathe before she read it. Opening it, something fell out on her lap. She would look at that in a moment but first she slowly read the letter.

He was a couple of years older than her. So far, she met what he was looking for. She could read, write, manage a household and was a woman of faith.

She picked up the piece that fell and realized that it was a picture. The man staring back at her was very a handsome man with a mustache, but it was his eyes that drew her in. Her heart rate sped up as she stared at his handsome eyes for a moment. Could he really be this handsome? Why wasn't he married already?

Getting up she retrieved a sheet of paper, quill and ink well. Her ankle hurt, but not as much as it did earlier. As she settled down to write to Cory, she wondered what she would write to him.

Dear Cory,

I do love to read good books. I have a couple of books that I kept that belonged to my father. I was trained up as a southern belle, my mother made sure of that.

I can manage a household, clean, cook, manage a garden and did more, especially when my parents were alive.

You requested a woman of faith. I am a woman of Christian faith. I attend church and read my

Bible. I will admit that my faith has been shaken a few times, but I still cling to Jesus.

In the South, things have been lean since the war. I am hoping to find a new home far from here.

I would love to know more about Virginia City, Nevada and about you.   Sincerely Etta.

Etta found a picture that her parents had taken of her before their death. It would have to work since it was all she had.

The next morning, Etta put the letter and the picture in an envelope. Pulling out another envelope she carefully put the contract in it and addressed it to Ester Davis.

Etta slowly made her way into town using her cane. Her ankle was much better this morning, but it still hurt. Using the cane helped her walk.

It would take a few days to heal but life didn't hold still for her.

Mr. Warren from the bank stopped her before she could head home. "You are running out of time. I have been patient with you, but I wouldn't wait much longer. You've had ample time to mourn. If you don't agree to marry me, you will force my hand. I have offered to let you stay in your home if you marry me. We can have the wedding, and I can move in. Just say the word."

Mr. Warren was an older man who not only wanted her family home but her. He made her skin crawl. Etta had managed to hold him off, but she wasn't sure how much longer she would be able to do that.

"It looks like you injured your ankle my dear. I will have my buggy brought around so I can personally take you home," Mr. Warren offered.

The sun was reflecting off of his bald head. He was old enough to be her father. Etta shivered at the thought of being in a carriage with him. She had to think fast. "It is just a little twist. I am on my way to Mabel's house. I'm sorry to disappoint you," Etta tried to explain as she prayed for help.

"Then we will just have to have dinner together soon. I must be getting back to the bank. I have a meeting," he said as he took his silver engraved pocket watch out of his vest pocket. Putting away his watch, he turned and left her standing.

Etta was still shaking as she turned and made her way to Mabel's house. It would be nice to sit for a few minutes and talk to her, if Mabel had time.

Mabel opened the door, "Good to see you, Etta. My goodness, it looks like you're hurt. Come in and sit down."

Etta answered her as she entered the house, "Good to see you too, Mabel. It's just a sprain. I will be fine in no time."

Mabel smiled at her friend and asked, "I hope you're right. What brought you to town?"

"I got a letter from a potential husband. I applied as a mail-order bride," Etta whispered. There were ears everywhere and she didn't want anyone other then her and her husband to know about it.

"Tell me about him," Mabel whispered back with a smile. She was excited for her friend as long as that was what she wanted.

"So far he sounds nice," Etta stated.

Mabel, "Well, that is good. I would hate to see you leave to marry someone who wouldn't be good to you."

"I'm running out of time here. Mr. Warren cornered me and he told me he was losing patience with me. He said he's not going to wait much longer for me to mourn my loss."

"That man gives me the willies, and he is not known for his patience or kindness," Mabel commented.

Etta echoed her statement, "I agree with you. Standing close to him makes me shake and I get a queasy stomach. I had better leave before he comes looking for me."

Mabel stood and said, "Wait. I have a little meat for you, and some bread. I'll wrap it quickly and you can sneak out the back door. If you would like me to drive you home, I can."

"No, thank you. He might see us on the road, and I would rather avoid him at all costs. I'm fine walking home. Going slower gives me time to forage and praise God. Thank you though. I do appreciate the thought," Etta said.

Mabel quickly gathered a few things and stuck them in her bag. "I don't want you to move far away, but I'd rather you do that then get stuck with Mr. Warren," Mabel said with a shiver.

Etta gave her friend a quick hug and said, "I'd rather live alone in the woods than marry that man. I will miss you. When I leave town, I will write to you."

Etta quietly slipped out of town. As she got closer to her home, she started humming a hymn. God had saved her from Mr. Warren again, even if it was only temporary.

As she entered her house she whispered, "Please God, rescue me from that man, if it is your will."

❦

Several weeks later, Etta found herself waiting for the next letter from Cory.

They had exchanged a couple letters, and she was hopeful. He sounded like a nice man. She would have to trust that the agency checked him out thoroughly. Etta prayed he wasn't a man who took to drinking alcohol and what he wrote was the truth in his letters.

But she feared her time here was running out. She didn't think she could delay Mr. Warren's plans much longer.

Paulette D. Marshall

The Railroad Tycoon Rescue

Chapter Five

The Waiting

Etta was finding it hard to wait for the next letter to arrive in the mail.

There was something about Cory that drew her in. It wasn't so much what he had said, but a feeling she got from his letters.

In Cory's first letter, he had asked for a picture of her. Luckily for her she had one that used to belong to her parents.

Etta often reread Cory's letters, and her heart sped up each time. She thought it was odd, but maybe there was something about Cory that reached her or it was the excitement of the possibility of something new.

One of his letters said,

I live with my grandmother and take care of her. Grandfather and Grandmother took care of me for years. Now it is my turn to take care of her.

Putting the letter down, she wondered how a thoughtful, attentive, good-looking man, could still be unmarried.

Cory sent a picture of himself dressed in western attire. She couldn't help but notice how handsome he was. But she shouldn't get her hopes up until she met him. What if he changed his mind and didn't want her?

The weeks between the letters were getting hard to handle, especially since Mr. Warren was being more persistent. He kept showing up at her house unannounced.

One time Etta just couldn't handle dealing with him, so she hid in the cellar. She was stuck in the cellar for an hour, but used the time to pray.

She was thankful that her ankle had quickly healed with no complications.

As she worked in the garden, Etta counted her blessings. Then she heard someone. Glancing behind her, she saw Mr. Warren. It was too late to hide. Her heart sank, but remembering her mother's lessons on being a proper southern lady, she squared her shoulders. "Good afternoon, Mr. Warren. Please sit down and I will bring out some refreshments."

Warren sat down on one of the chairs under the shade.

She brought out tea for the both of them. However, she had added a pinch of something special to Mr. Warren's tea. Hopefully, he wouldn't be staying long.

"This place could use some paint and work done on the house and barn. I can't wait to take over this home and make it into the southern home it should be, the home it once was," Mr. Warren stated in a condescending voice.

Etta held her tongue. There were many things she wanted to say to the man. To call him a gentleman would just be wrong, because he wasn't a gentleman at all. The only thing Etta could say was, "That would be nice." Hopefully she wouldn't be here to see it.

"I think we ought to set our wedding date. I see no need to wait much longer. I think two months from Sunday. That should give you ample time to prepare. I hope you have a suitable dress to wear to our wedding. After all, I own the bank and I'm a leader of this community." He took a big drink of his tea.

Etta almost choked on her tea that she was sipping. She managed to cough to cover it. Trying a different tactic, she said, "Are you sure? I mean, that sounds lovely. Its just Miss Spindle is a lovely young woman and you two seemed to get along so nicely. I thought you might be sweet on her and would ask for her hand."

"She is happy being my mistress, but don't worry there is enough of me for the two of you," Mr. Warren stated.

Paulette D. Marshall

Etta sat there stunned in silence. If she hadn't been trained by her mother, her mouth would have been open at Mr. Warren's statement. The cad. To sit there and announce his mistress to his future bride. Thank goodness she had slipped a little mayapple plant into his tea. She didn't feel as guilty as she did earlier. He would be in the outhouse a lot today.

Etta could tell that Warren was uncomfortable. He was pulling on his collar and squirming a little bit. The laxative was doing its job. He would have to run to the outhouse soon.

Squirming, with sweat pouring down his face, Mr. Warren said, "I just remembered an important meeting that I have. Our dinner will have to wait. The wedding will take place two months from Sunday." He stood up and hurried away to his carriage.

Etta hid a smile as she watched him retreat in haste. While she felt a pang of guilt, she reminded herself that it was his own fault for not respecting her boundaries. She didn't ask for his attention in the first place. It wasn't in her nature to harm anyone, but her knowledge of herbs and their uses had given her a quiet power to protect herself when needed. If she thought the shotgun could protect her from this man, she would use it, but in the end he would still take her house.

Over the years, many had come to her seeking herbal remedies. They often paid her in kind, offering food, meat, or even rare herbs in exchange for her medicine. It was one of the ways she had managed to survive on her own, relying on her skills and resources to make ends meet.

But with Mr. Warren now setting a date and tightening his grip on her future, Etta knew she would have to find a resolution, and quickly. The thought made her chest tighten, but she lifted her chin. She had faced challenges since her parents had passed and had managed to survive. She would find a way out of marrying Mr. Warren and a solution, just as she had every challenge.

Taking the teacups inside the house, she set them on the counter. As she washed dishes she thought of a plan.

Drying her hands, she sat down with a piece of paper and started a letter to Ester Davis. Maybe if she explained her situation, Ester could help her figure out a solution. If nothing else she would pack a bag and leave. Hopefully she could find work in another town. If she mailed the letter today, she might hear back before the wedding date. She planned to be gone before then.

Taking the letter and putting it in an envelope she quickly walked to town, praying that she wouldn't run into Mr. Warren again today.

That evening Etta counted her money and then sewed half of it into the bottom of her travel dress. She had enough to get to another town on a train. She wished she had more to last her until she found a job. Some of it had been used just to survive. She wished she could have paid off that loan when she found out about it, but it wasn't meant to be, so she had used a little of that money to survive.

Etta looked around the house, trying to figure out what she could take with her when she left. She walked into the bedroom and picked up her father's watch. Wrapping it in her mother's hanky to protect it and keep it safe, she gently set it in the carpet bag. She packed one of her father's books that she had read. There were a couple of other things that she put in the carpet bag so she wouldn't forget them if she had to leave in a hurry. There was more than enough room for her family Bible and her clothes. She hoped she would have time to pack before she had to leave, but with Mr. Warren demanding they marry she wasn't sure she would. Although, there wasn't much left in the house since she sold it.

The week went by as Etta worked around the house and yard. She wanted to take her tinctures, ointments, and herbs with her if she could. Of course, her herbal book would go with her. She was on pins and needles, hoping that Mr. Warren wouldn't drop by again. She was almost afraid to go out and work in her yard, but the weeds and two chickens couldn't wait.

The next week she received a letter from Cory. Opening the letter, she read it.

The Railroad Tycoon Rescue

Dear Etta,

You're a very beautiful young lady. I can't believe you're not already married.

We have exchanged a few letters already and I feel like we know a little bit about each other. I am hoping we can learn more about each other.

Here is a ticket if you would like to become my mail-order bride. If you don't, I will understand. But in case you do, I have enclosed extra money for food and anything else you might need for your trip.

If you choose not to be my mail-order bride, please return the money and ticket to me.

Sincerely, Cory.

Etta sat there for a moment. She thought that there would be more letters exchanged between them, yet in the light of her current situation she was very happy that she could leave before she was forced into marriage with Mr. Warren.

Taking a deep breath, she realized that God had answered her plea. "Thank you, Lord." It was odd being joyful and scared at the same time.

Now the tricky part would be how she could escape without Mr. Warren knowing she was leaving. She wanted to purchase some material to make a new dress, since Cory sent her a little extra money. After all, her dresses were extremely worn. Making the dress wouldn't take long and she couldn't show up in a thin, worn dress.

Maybe she could spend the night at Mabel's house the night before she left. That way she would be in town and could slip away early in the morning.

Etta worked everything out in her mind about how she was going to escape.

The next morning, she went into town and picked up a couple of things from the mercantile including material. It had been so long since she had a new dress that she took her time picking out the right material. She would only make one dress. She didn't want to spend too much money. It wouldn't be wise. She picked up five apples that she could take on the trip. She had a small chunk of cheese at home and half a loaf of bread she could put in her basket.

Etta walked to Mabel's house to explain her plan and ask for their help. She hated involving her in this, but she had no choice. To pull this off, she needed assistance. She would miss Mabel something awful and Mable's husband Mack.

"As much as I will miss you, Etta, I understand. Mack and I will do all we can to help you," Mabel assured her.

Mack said, "I will come by in the morning and pick you up. That way, you ladies can visit tomorrow before you leave. I will send your trunk off on the train. Just give me the name of town you are going."

Etta prayed for their safety, and said, "Thank you both. I just hope this will not get you in trouble or danger. I know Mr. Warren has a temper."

"Don't worry about us," Mabel assured her.

"I will protect her," Mack stated.

"I will continue to pray for your safety. I will miss you both terribly, but I can't marry that man."

"I don't think anyone wants to be with that man," Mabel said.

When Etta left their house, she felt better about her plan and prayed it would work. Hopefully, by the time she arrived in Nevada, Mr. Warren would give up finding her. At least she was praying for that.

Once at home, Etta cut out her new dress. She put it in her basket so that she could work on it later. Knowing that she could only take a few things so that it looked like she was coming back, she pulled out her steamer trunk that she had kept, and stood and looked around.

She needed her tinctures and ointments along with her herbs. If something should happen, these could help her survive and also help those in need. Picking up the first bottle, she carefully wrapped it with her apron, and laid it down on her parents' quilt that she had kept in the bottom of the trunk. Once her tinctures and ointments were inside, she carefully wrapped her mother's teacup in her mother's nice dress that she had kept. She could always trim the dress to fit herself if needed, but it was more of a reminder of her mother and the better times they had shared.

She packed a couple of small trinkets that she had saved. Standing, she looked around the room, then she walked into the kitchen and then her room. To anyone but her, that house still looked like she lived there. Oh, how she wished she could take a few more things with her, but she didn't want to take a chance that the banker would follow right behind her. She made sure she was just taking what was important to her.

Once the trunk held everything she was taking with her, she gently set the hanging herbs she was still drying on top.

Next, she packed what clothes she would need to take into her carpet bag. She would leave her thin dress on the peg when she left, that way it would look like she was coming back. She would wear her travel dress and use her nightgown.

Taking her letters from Cory, she put them in her basket. She wrapped a piece of ribbon around the letters. In the morning, she would add the food and water to her basket.

Tomorrow when Mack picked her up to take her to town, she would take her two chickens and

The Railroad Tycoon Rescue

rooster to Mabel's house. After all, Mabel and Mack made sure to share food with her, and she knew they could use a couple of chickens. It would be a nice gift for them.

After dinner since she didn't have anything to do, Etta sat down and started sewing her new dress. Staying up late, she had her dress over halfway finished. She anticipated she could work on it on the train. That would also give her time to add a few extra details to it. She found some lace that she was saving that would be pretty on her dress.

It seemed like everything was falling into place. At least she was praying it was.

❦

Etta got up early in the morning. She used most of the flour she had left and made a loaf of bread. She wasn't sure how long the trip would take but she was hoping that the food she was taking would last the whole trip to Nevada. She boiled the eggs she gathered so she could take those too.

Etta put the hard-boiled eggs, cheese, apples, and the wrapped loaf of bread with a couple of big jars filled with water into the basket.

After her breakfast of oatmeal, Etta wrote a note for Mr. Warren. She would have someone deliver it to the bank after she left.

Mr. Warren,

Paulette D. Marshall

I am going to Sweet Water to get material for my wedding dress. I have a better chance at finding just the right material in a bigger town that has more choices. If I can't find it, I will order it, so I might be gone a few days.

Etta

Etta was praying the letter would hold him off, at least for a bit.

When Mack arrived to pick her up, she was ready. They loaded a few jars of food that she had in the cellar and then the chickens. Mack loaded her trunk in the back. Etta took one last look around at her home. She hated leaving anything in the house, but she knew she had to make her story sound real. She reminded herself that the most important things she took along with her were memories. Her parents wouldn't want her to marry Mr. Warren.

Her father had called Mr. Warren a cad too. Which made her wonder what her father knew about him.

Even though she was frightened of what lay ahead, she trusted God to see her through. But the question that kept haunting her was: would she escape, or would she get caught before she even left town?

Chapter Six

The Journey

The visit with Mabel had been bittersweet. Etta and Mabel enjoyed the day talking and working. In the evening, they worked on Etta's dress together. It wouldn't take Etta long to finish hemming it. Mabel had given her more lace and helped sew it on. They tried to enjoy their limited time together since they didn't know when they would see each other again.

"I promise to write and tell you everything," Etta said.

"That might not be a good idea. I would wait at least a month. Otherwise, Mr. Warren might try to find you. We have all heard what a vindictive man he can be," Mabel shared.

Etta shivered. She had heard those rumors too, but she was praying that wasn't true.

Mabel stood and said, "We'd best get to bed, even though it's early. I can tell you're tired and you will leave early in the morning."

"You're right. Good night," Etta said, feeling a little sad. She didn't want the evening to end, but she knew her friend was right, and she had to be at the train station very early in the morning to catch the first train out of town. Hopefully, before anyone saw her.

Etta hurried to the station a few minutes before the train would pull out. They didn't want to get there too early. Pulling her shawl tight against the slight chill in the air, she was grateful to be leaving before winter set in. Mabel walked beside her, but they had already said their goodbyes, knowing this was the hardest part of the plan. It wasn't just a short trip to look for a wedding dress material, as they wanted everyone else to believe. It was the beginning of her escape.

Mack had already taken her steamer trunk ahead of time, carefully labeling it with Cory's name. Etta hoped there wouldn't be any issues with that but, they couldn't risk using her real name. In such a small town, news would travel fast, and someone was bound to run straight to Mr. Warren.

At the station, she gave Mabel a quick hug, managing a tight smile before boarding the train on trembling legs. Every second, she braced herself, waiting for someone to stop her, to demand where she was going or tell her she couldn't leave. But no one did.

Thank goodness that Cory had sent her a ticket and that she didn't have to purchase it.

The Railroad Tycoon Rescue

She found an empty seat on the train. Once seated, she waved to her friend trying to appear happy. She had her travel suit on with her hat and had the lace veil pulled down which hid her face at least some. Once out of sight of the station and town, Etta wiped away a few tears. She promised herself she would enjoy this journey.

Etta had proven to herself that she was stronger than she had thought she was once her parents had passed. It was just like her father had said, "With the Lord standing with you, there isn't anything you can't do. Depend on Him to lead you and listen to Him." It was as if she could hear him saying it to her right now.

Bowing her head, she silently thanked the Lord for getting her out of town safely, before Mr. Warren found out. She added a prayer for her husband to be.

Etta looked through the train windows at the scenery.

As the train picked up speed, she slowly relaxed. A part of her kept waiting for someone to ride up to the train and demand that she return to town.

The conductor asked for her ticket, and after she handed it to him, she asked, "How long until I reach my destination?"

"About two weeks ma'am, barring any bad weather or issues," the conductor said before he moved on.

Paulette D. Marshall

It took her a while to relax, though she wouldn't fully feel at ease until she was married to Cory. A part of her wondered if she should tell him about Mr. Warren. But what if Cory believed that Mr. Warren had some kind of prior claim on her? The thought unsettled her even more. Hopefully Ester got her letter that she sent and explained everything that was going on. She had a feeling that Ester would be able to help her. After all, Ester's letter had told her to write if she needed anything.

That first day was exciting, but soon that excitement diminished some. Sleeping sitting upright on the hard bench was challenging, to say the least not to mention being covered in coal dust. Etta soon missed walking around. There was so little space to stretch her legs. Although the changing scenery was beautiful.

On one of the stops, an older lady stopped by Etta and asked, "Good afternoon, may I sit here?"

"Yes, please," Etta responded.

"My name is Mrs. Moore, but you can call me Jane."

Etta smiled and said, "Nice to meet you. My name is Etta."

"I'm on the way home after visiting my daughter and her family. I had a wonderful time, but it will be nice to be home. The train is so much better than the stagecoach was."

The Railroad Tycoon Rescue
"Sounds like you had a good time," Etta said.

"Those little ones were rambunctious, but I enjoyed my time with them," Jane said.

The first week seemed to go by quickly. Reading the Bible and looking out the window helped pass the time, and so did working on her dress. Once the dress was finished, she decided to embroider the front of the button area.

She had seen some beautiful scenery. From tall mountains that took her breath away, to trees that were trying to reach the sky and then the vast prairies. The endless beauty of the leaves changing their colors. Winter wasn't too far away. She had seen some snow on the highest mountain tops, which were breathtaking. God sure created some beautiful sights for her.

At the beginning of the second week, Etta's food supply and water were getting low, even though she had tried to ration it. She had no choice. She needed to get off and get more supplies. Etta had noticed at many of the train stops there were people selling food and water at the station. Several people got off and purchased something, and then quickly returned.

Etta got off at one stop to buy a chunk of cheese and a couple slices of bread. She was in luck when she saw the hard-boiled eggs for sale and bought three. There was a bucket of water and she refilled her jars.

Paulette D. Marshall

What she wouldn't give for a good night's sleep, clean clothes, hot food, and most importantly a bath. She hadn't felt this dirty before. She regretted that she would have to meet her future husband looking like this.

Jane sitting next to her made the journey more pleasant with their light conversation. It also provided a sense of protection from the occasional gentlemen who tried to catch her attention or stared at her a little too long. Jane wasn't afraid to sound her displeasure in a firm yet kind way.

When Jane left the train a few days before Etta was to arrive at Virginia City, Etta put her carpet bag on the seat next to her, to discourage any male from asking to sit next to her. She looked through the windows at the ever-changing scenery.

Etta would miss Jane's company. There had been so many changes in her life the last couple of years, and several goodbyes. How much could a person take?

A few stops later, a lovely older lady asked to sit there.

"My name is Miss Miller, but please call me Cora," the older woman said.

"Nice to meet you. My name is Miss Dixon, but please call me Etta."

Cora wasn't very talkative, but that was fine with Etta. She was tired and dirty.

The Railroad Tycoon Rescue

The scenery had become drier, and trees had become sparse. In fact, the trees were replaced by tall looking things, which looked strange to her. They looked like they would poke someone. She couldn't wait to see them up close. She overheard someone calling them cactus.

Etta was happy when she saw a few trees again. She was curious about the cactus and wondered what medical purpose cactus had and if it was edible.

Taking out her herbal book that her grandmother and great-grandmother had written. Etta looked in it to see if there was anything on cactus. There was a mention, but not a lot of information about them. That would be one of the things she wanted to find out more about and their medicinal purpose. Usually something that defended themselves that aggressively had some great medicinal purposes

The conductor announced, "For those of you who are traveling to Virginia City, Nevada, we will be arriving this afternoon."

Etta tried to dust off some of the coal dust that seemed to be embedded in her clothes.

"I don't think that is going to help, dearie. I am sure whoever is going to meet you will understand. Thank goodness your travel suit is navy blue. It doesn't look too bad," Cora said with a kind smile.

Etta smiled and said, "Thank you, that's kind of you to say."

The conductor announced as he walked, "We will be pulling into Virginia City in thirty minutes, folks."

Etta couldn't wait. The end was almost here. She knew it was silly, but she picked up her carpet bag and held it. Her basket was still sitting on the floor.

After a while the train gave a small, unsettling wiggle, something it hadn't done before. Then it began to sway, back and forth, the movement growing more violent. Just as Etta started to feel alarmed, a deafening crunch shattered the air, the sound sharp and painful to her ears. Moments later, an ear-piercing screech echoed through the railcar.

Passengers were thrown in every direction. Etta clung tightly to her carpet bag, heart pounding as she squeezed her eyes shut and prayed. Was this how her life would end?

The Railroad Tycoon Rescue

Chapter Seven

Counting blessings

When Etta finally managed to open her eyes, her vision was blurry, and nothing around her made sense. Her head throbbed, and her body ached as she struggled to focus. She could hear distant screams and cries, but the world seemed disjointed. She realized she was lying on the floor in the railcar, which used to be the side of the railcar, surrounded by shattered glass that glittered in the faint light.

Why was there glass everywhere?

Blinking, she began to piece everything together in her mind, the train was on its side, twisted and mangled. Panic surged through her as she spotted Cora, crumpled not far away. Desperate, Etta tried to crawl toward her, only then realizing that she was still clinging tightly to her carpet bag.

As she made her way to Cora, she saw her move. "Cora, are you ok?" Etta's voice came out in a mere whispered.

"I think I'm ok. Although I'm really not sure. What happened?" Cora asked.

Etta set her bag down and checked Cora's head. "We were in a train accident. I think you bumped your head."

"That would explain why it hurts so bad," Cora said as she tried to get up.

"Just stay there. It may take a bit before the world stops spinning. I need to see if I can help the others," Etta said. Picking up her bag, she made her way around the car. Good thing it wasn't full.

There were more serious injuries. Etta tore the bottom of her petticoat off and wrapped it around a man's bleeding arm. When she looked up, Cora was beside her.

"Cora, could you watch him? I need to go see if I can help the others. There's bound to be some seriously injured people who need attention," Etta said, her voice steady despite everything that had gone on.

"I've got his. Go ahead. I'll come help if I can," Cora replied, nodding in understanding.

Etta got up and started praying. She had to try to get out of this rail car and help those who were injured. If only she had all her medicinal medicines. She prayed there was a doctor on board to help with the injured.

Finally finding a hole in the side of the car, she managed to shimmy out of it, tearing her travel dress in the process and scraping herself.

The Railroad Tycoon Rescue

Glancing down at the ripped fabric, she realized it was her last nice dress, but that hardly mattered now.

The confusion and destruction around her was overwhelming. Part of the train was a twisted mess of metal, and the car before hers was in ruins, though it looked like there might still be survivors inside.

Etta made her way toward the wreckage, searching for an opening. A few bodies were scattered around, thrown from the train. She could see a couple of people already helping others. Spotting someone lying still outside the car, she knelt down and pressed her ear to their chest, but heard nothing. Saying a quick prayer for them, she continued on, determined to reach the car.

She found a small gap and squeezed through, her heart pounding as she saw the destruction and devastation inside. A woman was trapped beneath a heavy bench, crying out for help. Etta pushed against the bench, surprised at how heavy it truly was, but somehow she managed to move it. Nearby, a man with a stethoscope and a black bag, was helping someone else.

As soon as the bench was clear, Etta began aiding the injured woman until the doctor joined her and took over. Not lingering on those beyond help, she offered a silent prayer for them and kept moving. More people soon arrived to assist.

The most heartbreaking were a couple of injured children. Etta wished she had her herbal medicine with her to help, but she knew that some people didn't believe in the power of their healing. God created the earth and everything on it. He surely knew what he was doing when he created medicinal plants.

The injuries in this car were severe, but as Etta glanced toward the next car, it looked far worse. There didn't seem to be any survivors in that wreckage. Thank goodness she hadn't been in a different car. Though her car had its share of injuries, it had faired much better than the others. Etta wondered about the engine. She didn't remember seeing it, although she hadn't been looking for it either.

Etta overheard the conductor saying, "When the train doesn't arrive on time, they will be concerned. First, they are going to send a telegram to the town of Caliente and see if the train had arrived there on time. After finding out that the train did indeed stop there and it was on time, they will send out someone to look for us. It's just a matter of time before help arrives. We just need to hang on until then."

Etta prayed that was true. Whatever else they said she didn't hear because the conductor moved away.

Cora tapped on her shoulder and said, "There is a woman in our car that is in labor. I get the impression you know more about medical issues than I do."

"I might, but I am sure the doctor knows more," Etta admitted.

"If it's not an emergency and you can handle it, young lady, I would appreciate it. My time could be better used helping those injured," the doctor said.

"I think Cora and I can handle it. If there is a complication though I will send Cora to fetch you," Etta said as she got up and swayed a little bit.

"Be careful. You probably have a concussion," the doctor advised her.

"I'm sure most of us, if not all of us, have a concussion from what we have been through," Etta said. Turning, she slowly walked away, following Cora. They made their way back to their car. The woman was in pain, that much was obvious. Most everyone had moved out of the car to give the woman some privacy.

"That little one is ready to be out in this world. My name is Etta. Cora and I will do our best to help you bring your little one safely in to this world so you can hold them," Etta said as she knelt down by her.

"My name is Lucy," the woman said.

"When did the pains start?" Etta asked.

"Early this morning," the Lucy admitted.

Etta inquired, "Is your husband traveling with you?"

"No, he isn't," she said.

Etta helped Lucy bring her child into the world without boiling water or her herbs. She quickly lost track of time as she helped the mother.

"Cora, could you bring me my carpet bag? We can use my nightgown to wrap the baby in. I think I might have some herbs in my bag to help too," Etta asked.

Etta found her scissors and cut the cord, tying it off with thread. What would she have done if she hadn't had her bag? She didn't want to think about that, especially since her head already hurt. Instead, she whispered her thanks to God, knowing He was supplying her every need. Philippians 4:19, But my God shall supply all your need according to his riches in glory by Christ Jesus.

Etta gently wrapped the healthy baby in her nightgown. She pulled out the herbs she had packed, offering them to the mother. "These will have to do. They will help with the cramps and help you heal. I'm sorry I don't have any way to make tea out of these, and they will be a little bitter. I wish I could get to my trunk for the rest of my herbs, but I don't think that's possible."

Suddenly, someone shouted, "Fire!"

The Railroad Tycoon Rescue

Two injured men rushed into the car. "Sorry, ma'am," one said, "but we need to clear everyone out and quickly. There's a fire near what's left of the engine." One of them carefully lifted the mother and baby, carrying them out.

Etta grabbed her carpet bag, and followed, squeezing through the hole in the side of the car. It wasn't easy, but everyone made it out safely, moving quickly away from the burning wreckage.

Where was the help? Surely, enough time already passed, and the rescuers should be on their way here.

Once they were at a safe distance, the survivors gathered and discussed what to do next. A man volunteered to head toward Virginia City, hoping to meet up with their rescuers. Many were too injured to walk.

Etta wished she could take some herbs for her headache but since there was very little water there was no chance of that. The good news was that the baggage car had disconnected and was a way from the rest of the train. Etta was praying that her herbs were undamaged.

This was not how she had imagined the day would go. Exhausted, Etta longed to lie down and rest, but there were too many people who still needed help. So, she kept moving, forcing herself to stay busy. The doctor was in high demand.

Paulette D. Marshall

Cory had paced up and down the boardwalk. The train was already half an hour late. He would give it ten more minutes and then he was going to contact the conductor. The train was usually on time. He couldn't shake the feeling that something wasn't right. He felt bad that the pastor and his wife were waiting to conduct the wedding ceremony.

Feeling a growing sense of worry, Cory approached the door of the train station and stepped inside. "George, have you heard anything? What happened to the train?" he asked, his voice laced with concern.

"No, sir. I just sent a telegram, and I should hear back," George replied, his words barely finished when the telegraph machine began tapping.

After translating the message George glanced at the message and said, "The train arrived at Caliente right on time."

"That means something must have happened, either an accident or robbery," Cory said his voice tense. He turned in time to see Malcom step into the train station.

"From what I just overheard, it looks like we'll need to invoke the rescue clause," Malcom said. "I'll notify the other mail-order husbands that it's in effect. We'll have a posse assembled in no time. I'll also get Lucas and Sheriff since they're part of the clause." With that, he turned and left the office.

The Railroad Tycoon Rescue

Cory was glad he had decided to bring the buckboard into town to pick up Etta. He chose it because he wasn't sure how much luggage she'd have and didn't want her to see his fancy buggy just yet.

After a moment's thought, he headed to the mercantile, realizing they might need lanterns and extra blankets in case there had been an accident. Once inside, he gathered a couple lanterns, blankets, extra ammunition, and a pair of water skins.

"Storing up for a storm, Cornelius?" Willbur asked as he watched him grab supplies.

"The train hasn't arrived yet, but it reached Caliente on time," Cory explained, his voice tinged with concern and a hint of fear. "It's either been held up or there's been an accident. We're gathering a posse. Those people could be hurt and waiting for help."

"I will shut my doors as soon as you've got everything you need and join the posse," Wilbur offered.

"Thank you, Willbur. Please put these on my tab," Cory replied.

"Will do," Wilbur said with a nod. "I'll grab some jerky, my saddlebag, and a water skin to bring along. Let me get my horse."

Cory said, "Good idea about the jerky. Who knows how long we will be out there. I have some in my saddle bag in the wagon, but we might need more."

By the time Cory finished gathering his supplies and loading them onto the buckboard, several men with their horses had gathered outside the mercantile, ready to ride.

Sheriff John was in front of the sheriff's office talking to his deputies. A few men and horses were gathered there too.

Cory mounted his buckboard and moved it closer to the sheriff's office. He was ready to move out and he knew that every minute was important if someone was injured.

"Cory, we are almost ready. Just waiting for a couple more men. We mail-order bride husbands stick together."

Annette stepped out of her house carrying a large basket and approached her husband, John. "Annette, you can put that basket of food in Cory's wagon, if that is ok with you, Cory?"

Cory tipped his hat at Annette and answered, "That's fine, John, and thank you, Annette."

A man walked up to Cory. "Can I grab a ride with you, Cory?"

Looking down, Cory saw Lucas leading his horse.

The Railroad Tycoon Rescue

"Sure thing, Lucas. Glad to have you next to me. Who's running your restaurant?" Cory asked as Lucas tied his horse to the back of the wagon.

Lucas climbed up and settled next to Cory. "My beautiful bride, Rosabella, is handling things. I told her she could close up for the night if it got to be too much. But I had to come. Duty calls. Honestly, I never thought we'd actually need to invoke the rescue clause," Lucas said with a shake of his head. "I hope no one is hurt too bad."

Annette, standing nearby, chimed in, "Don't worry Lucas, I'll help my sister with the restaurant. I'm sure we'll manage just fine. And we'll all be praying for you all."

Lucas nodded gratefully. "There's nothing like a small town pulling together."

Another man approached the wagon. "Mind if I join you? You may need an extra pair of hands and my assistance."

"Pastor Jones, we'd be glad to have you," Cory said as Lucas scooted over to make room. "And you're right, we might need your help. Still, I'm praying it won't come to that."

Cory turned back to Sheriff John. "I'm heading out now. It won't take you long to catch up on horseback."

Without another word, Cory flicked the reins, urging the buckboard forward. The horses responded with a quick trot, their hooves clattering against the dirt road. A gnawing sense of unease settled in his chest, an inexplicable weight he couldn't shake. Something was wrong. He couldn't explain how he knew, but the certainty of it pressed down on him like a storm cloud.

Every instinct told him they needed to hurry. The thought of injured passengers or a possible robbery made his grip on the reins tighten. Glancing at Lucas and Pastor Jones besides him, he saw the same tension mirrored in their faces. This wasn't just a routine ride; it was the beginning of something far more serious.

Chapter Eight

The Rescue

Cory waved to the men behind him as he urged the horses forward. Time was slipping away, and darkness would fall before they knew it. He guided the buckboard toward the railroad tracks, keeping the pace steady at a trot. Pushing the horses too hard would only exhaust them, and they needed to conserve their strength for whatever lay ahead.

Although his team of thoroughbreds was strong and capable, Cory couldn't help but wish he'd left the wagon behind and ridden one of the horses instead. But the wagon might prove essential, especially if they had injured passengers or worse. He just hoped someone else would think to bring another wagon just in case.

Cory drove in silence for a while, his eyes scanning the horizon. Suddenly he squinted and leaned forward. "I think I see someone walking up ahead. Do you see him, Lucas?"

Lucus shifted in his seat, narrowing his eyes as he focused on the figure in the distance. "Yeah, I see him," he replied, his tone laced with concern. "That's not a good sign."

Cory suggested, "We won't know what happened until we talk to him. I just pray everyone is ok."

"I have been praying," Pastor Jones stated.

"This must be hard for you since you own the railroad, and you have a mail-order bride riding it," Lucas remarked.

Cory admitted, "Yes, it is, but Etta doesn't know that I own the railroad, at least not yet. I was going to tell her before we married."

"I'm glad. It wasn't right not telling her before she agreed to marry you," Pastor Jones commented.

"I agree, but I had my reasons," Cory voiced.

"I am sure you did," pastor Jones said. "Remember the saying, oh what a tangled web we weave, when first we practice to deceive? That isn't the way to start a new relationship or a marriage. Remember the Bible verse Leviticus 19:11. 'Do not steal. Do not lie. Do not deceive one another.' And that is the last thing I will say about it."

The man walking toward them was now much closer. As they pulled up beside him, Cory got a better look and felt a jolt of alarm. The man looked terrible as if he'd been through something harrowing. His clothes were filthy and torn, stained with what appeared to be dried blood. There was even a smudge of crimson near his head, and his face was etched with exhaustion and despair.

"Thank you, Lord. I thought I was going to have to walk all the way to town for help," the man said.

"Here, have a drink of water," Cory said as he offered him a water skin. Pastor Jones moved to the back of the wagon. "Why don't you climb up and you can tell us what happened as we ride," Corry suggested. He was sure they were needed at the train, wherever it was at, and he didn't want to waste time.

The man held on to the water skin and climbed up into the wagon.

Corry flicked his wrist, moving the horses as soon as the man sat down. "Train wreck. Many hurt," the man said and then took a drink of the water.

"Easy with the water. Too much and you might be sick," Malcom suggested.

Cory asked, his voice laced with concern, "How bad is the train wreck?"

"Pretty bad. The engine and the first couple of cars took the blunt of it, but the third car and the luggage weren't too bad. Although I'm not sure how they are now since I left right after the fire started." He took another sip of water.

Cory had been praying silently as he drove, but now his prayers became desperate pleas especially for Etta. His heart ached with worry, and every bounce of the wagon seemed to echo the urgency of his thoughts.

Up ahead, something bright caught his eye. Squinting, he tried to make out what it was- a flicker of firelight, perhaps? Or lanterns? As he prayed for everyone involved, a heavy realization settled over him: this was his railroad. He was responsible for the passengers, the crew, and the safety of everyone on that train.

His mind raced, sifting through every precaution he'd put in place, every safety measure he'd insisted upon. Had they missed something? Could he have done more? The weight of it pressed down on him, but he shook it off. Now wasn't the time for doubt.

In his mind, Cory began running through everything that would need to be done. If there were injuries, they'd need medical supplies and a way to transport the wounded. If the tracks were damaged, repairs would have to be quickly made to prevent further delays.

The list felt endless, but Cory pushed down the rising anxiety. Once step at a time, he told himself. First, they had to reach the train and figure out exactly what they were dealing with.

Again, he wished that he was on his horse so he could quickly find out about his mail-order bride. He felt the weight of it all.

The Railroad Tycoon Rescue

Malcom grabbed Cory on the shoulder and said, "It's not your fault. Don't think the worst before we can see it. Keep the faith."

Cory nodded, but didn't say anything. The weight of responsibility and the unknown sat on his shoulders. As they got closer, Cory sped the horses up. He could hear the other horses behind him. The bright light got brighter, and he could see dark smoke billowing up. He saw what looked like people in front of the fire. The black smoke rose from what seemed like a pile of metal. Cory's heart sank.

The closer Cory got, the drier his throat became. He could make out people scattered across the ground, some laying down, others kneeling over them, trying to offer comfort or aid. The wreckage of the engine and railcars came into focus, and his heart nearly stopped at the sight. The twisted metal and debris painted a grim picture, and he silently pleaded with God for his bride's safety. But he would have to wait to find her. The injured needed to be taken care of first.

As they neared the passengers, Cory halted the wagon. Though it felt like an eternity since they'd set out to help, in truth, they'd arrived as quickly as possible.

He could hear voices, some talking, others crying, and the occasional scream. As Cory dismounted, a few of the survivors came up to him, looking for guidance and dazed. He knew he needed to get the injured to town quickly and assess the scene. They would need an investigator to determine what had caused the wreck. Was the train going too fast, or was there another explanation?

Malcom was by his side, steady and ready. "Malcom, we need to get the most severely injured back to town as quickly as possible," Cory said, noting Pastor Jones nearby.

"I can take the first load in your wagon, while you attend to what needs to be done here. Or one of the other men can drive, and I can stay to help you," Malcom offered.

Cory nodded. "I'd rather have you here with me. One of the men on horseback can drive my wagon with a load of injured." Cory was glad that Malcom was with him. Having a lawyer by his side might be a good idea.

He bent down to help the first injured passenger, a railroad worker, who looked up at him with weary eyes. "Sir, it was awful," the man said, voice trembling.

"Matthew, I'll have questions for you soon, but first, how are you doing?"

"I'm in pain, but I know there are those who need help more than me," Matthew said.

"Don't worry, Matthew, we will have the doctor in town take care of you," Cory said and moved to stand.

"Sir, there is a doctor here somewhere. He's been helping everyone he can. I think he was riding in the back car," Matthew said before pain overtook him.

"You just rest. We will find him," Cory assured him. "Malcom, let's start organizing the passengers. The ones who need attention now should be loaded. You might check with the doctor too. I am sure he already knows who should be moved out first. That is, if we can find him. And let's keep an eye out for those who need help too."

Cory looked up as more help arrived. He continued to work, checking on the injured and looking for the doctor. The fire in the engine still concerned him, even though it was a distance away it was still too close for comfort. The wagon had several people in it by the time they found the doctor who was working on a patient. When he finished, the doctor looked up. "It is good to see help."

"We came as fast as we could when the train didn't show up. We have already gathered a few of the injured into a wagon, those who we thought should go first. I think our town doctor is in another wagon on his way here. When he knows you're here, he will return with the injured," Cory said.

"Good. I can point out the ones who need to go now," the doctor said.

"I will have them transported. We might have to wait for more wagons," Cory said.

"We will do the best we can do with what we have," doc said.

Cory looked at the woman who had been helping the doctor. She looked beautiful, even in her torn, dirty clothes. She had no hat on, and her hair was half out of her bun. Cory noticed all of that with one quick look, but he didn't have time to look further. He had to help get people loaded and make sure Doc Hendricks was on the wagon with the injured, if he had made it here.

The next couple of hours went by quickly, helping those in need and loading the injured. There were a few that were walking around injured, and they would take the last wagon. Cory wasn't sure where Etta was, and he hadn't had time to ask anyone. He was worried sick over not knowing if she was ok or injured. Had he already talked to her and had not realized it? Even though he had a picture, it was an older one and he didn't have time to keep checking it.

After sending several wagons filled with injured people, there were still a few people left waiting to be taken to town. That should fill at least a wagon if not two.

Cory asked, "I am looking for Etta. Do any of you know where she is?"

Etta was beyond exhausted. Her head was pounding, and she had ringing in her ears. She

The Railroad Tycoon Rescue

figured she had a concussion, but that didn't stop her from helping others. She couldn't remember the last time she had a drink of water, let alone when she last ate. Her legs were starting to wobble but she wouldn't stop. People needed help. She heard her name, but she was concentrating on the lady whom she was praying with. She had been helping the doctor and praying with anyone who wanted or needed prayer, especially those critically injured. They had lost several lives, but she thanked God it wasn't worse. She wanted to make sure each person had a chance to ask God into their heart if they didn't already know him.

As she got up to walk her legs gave out from underneath her.

Paulette D. Marshall

The Railroad Tycoon Rescue

Chapter Nine

Joining of Two Hearts

Etta knew the moment her legs gave out. There was nothing she could do. As she started falling, strong arms caught her before she hit the ground. "Ma'am, are you ok?" a deep voice asked. She looked up into the darkest green eyes she had ever seen. Etta blinked, mesmerized.

Cory could only stare into the most beautiful deep blue eyes he had ever seen.

After a few minutes of looking into each other's eyes, Etta became aware that he had asked her name. "My name is Etta," she whispered.

"Etta. Are you injured?" Cory asked.

"She has a mild concussion and a few minor injuries," the doctor assured them as he came up next to them. "She has been a great help to me. I am sure she is as worn out as I am, if not more since she isn't used to handling so many injuries. Young lady, if you ever want a job as a nurse, I hope you look me up. I will give you the job. You know your herbal medicines, not to mention bandaging."

"That is high praise," Cory said with a smile as he looked down at the beautiful woman in his arms. "Thank you, miss, for your help or is it misses.?"

"Thank you, Doc Hendricks. I will keep that in mind," Etta replied softly, fighting the overwhelming urge to give in to the exhaustion. She wanted nothing more than to lie down and sleep, and being in a stranger's arms felt strange. On the one hand, it felt wonderful and she was so tired, yet it wasn't her intended. She was not accustomed to strangers holding her. What would her intended think if he saw her like this, held by a man she barely knew?

"Sir, if you could please set me down," Etta said. "For one thing, I don't even know your name and for another I'm sure my intended would not be happy if he saw this."

"Intended?" Cory said as his heart seemed to speed up. Could this lovely woman be his Etta?

No one said anything for a moment or two and then Cory said, "I was worried you were hurt in the train wreck. My name is Cory. I had thought our meeting would be a little different. It's a pleasure to finally meet you, Etta. I have been praying for you and your well-being." He tipped his head toward her.

"Forgive me for not removing my hat. Seems my arms are full."

The Railroad Tycoon Rescue

Etta blinked. Even though this man was dirty and tired, he was still very handsome and now he was telling her he was her intended. Etta explained. "I was in the last car. The luggage car was behind me. I am thankful that I didn't decide to sit elsewhere, but I feel a little guilty."

Pastor Jones walked up to Cory. "Cory, this looks like the last load. I see you have your hands full. I thought we got all of the seriously injured out with the last wagon.

"Pastor Jones, I would like you to meet my intended, Etta Dixon."

"I am happy to meet you. Are you ok?" Pastor Jones asked in concern.

"I am fine. Really, you can put me down. It's just been a long day," Etta insisted.

"You almost collapsed," Cory said gently. "The Doctor just mentioned how exhausted you are, not to mention the concussion. You've done more than enough. I'll set you in the wagon now, since most of the injured have been loaded."

"With all those injured, and the sick in town, tomorrow is liable to be very busy and we'll have burials to handle too," Pastor Jones said gently. "I don't mean to be insensitive, but I'd suggest marrying you both right now. It may be several days, if not longer, before I can get to it otherwise. With the hotel sure to be full, it wouldn't be right for you to take her back to your home, even with your grandmother there. I would prefer to join you both in holy matrimony now."

Now that he had seen his intended, he didn't want to wait to marry her. Cory looked down at the lovely woman still in his arms. "Etta, I know this isn't an ideal wedding, but I understand Pastor Jones's point. He will be needed. But if you want to wait and marry whenever he has a chance to fit us in, we can wait," Cory asked.

"It was my understanding that we would be wed after I arrived in town but after what has happened …." Etta couldn't seem to finish her sentence. All she could say was, "I guess we better do it now." She worried she must look terrible and she could feel some of her hair on her shoulders.

"We will need two witnesses," Pastor Jones insisted as he looked around.

"I would like a moment to at least fix my hair," Etta whispered to Cory.

"You're very beautiful just the way you are. Let me set you down. Do you think you can stand?" Cory offered.

Etta replied, "Yes, I think I will be fine and I would prefer to get married standing up."

Gently setting her on her feet, Cory watched her closely.

Etta felt her hair and realized that some of her hairpins were missing. Putting her hair back up might not be an option, especially without a mirror.

Cory watched her for a moment and then said, "Please, let me help you." He started pulling out her hairpins and he stuck them in his pocket. It only took him a moment and her hair hung down around her face and down her back. "You are so beautiful."

Etta looked deep into Cory's eyes, and she saw something there that she wanted to know more about. She also saw a hint he was hiding something but what he was hiding she had no clue. She just prayed that it wasn't something bad. She had seen how caring he could be to other people. He was treated with respect. His clothes were dirty but the material was of nice quality, which seemed odd to her. She remembered when she used to have tailored clothes herself. Her travel suit was tailored at one time, but that was before she lost weight. She was just too tired to think.

Pastor Jones had two people as witness to their marriage.

Malcom walked up to Cory and said, "The other wagon is on the way to town. I thought it would be best to get everyone there."

"Thank you. That was the right thing to do. Pastor Jones is going to perform the ceremony and then we will head to town," Cory said.

"Good thing I stayed behind. I don't want to miss your wedding. Ester is going to be upset that she missed it and I can think of a couple others who will be too," Malcom stated.

"We will have a reception so no one will feel left out," Cory offered.

Malom nodded his head.

Cory had tried to get a minute alone with Etta, but he didn't get a chance to explain about his name or his wealth yet. He hated to start this marriage with a secret, but it looked like they were. He had his arm around Etta to help support her. She was leaning against him, just a little.

This wasn't how Etta had pictured her wedding but at least it was beautiful outside.

Pastor Jones said, "We are gathered together to join this man and woman in holy matrimony."

Etta turned and looked at Cory. He was quite handsome and strong. He had lifted her like she weighed nothing.

"Do you Cornelius Vanderbilt Jr., take Etta Sue Dixon to be your lawful wife?"

Etta had stopped listening at that point. Cornelius? Vanderbilt? Her mouth must have fallen open. But he said his name was Cory? She silently struggled.

The Railroad Tycoon Rescue

Corry whispered in her ear, "I promise to explain everything to you. Can we just proceed with the wedding?"

If Etta didn't have the possibility of someone following her and danger, she might have waited to get married, but she didn't have that luxury.

Etta looked at him and then whispered, "You're not wanted by the law or anything bad, are you?" She noticed that the pastor was standing there silently. He must be waiting for something.

"No, I am not," Cory whispered back as he waited.

The name Vanderbilt sounded very familiar. Where had she heard it before? Then it hit her. She had read about the wealthy Vanderbilt family.

Cory watched Etta closely, and he could tell the moment she realized who he was. Her eyes widened in surprise, but she quickly composed herself, her expression smoothing into calm reserve. Though he longed for a moment alone with her to talk, he knew now wasn't the time. They were needed back in town. People were counting on him and Pastor Jones. There were injured to tend to, families waiting for news, and too many lives upended by this tragic accident.

He glanced over at her again, feeling the weight of not telling her everything. If only they had a quiet moment together, but that would have to wait. Right now, there was simply too much to do.

Etta shifted her gaze from Cory to Pastor Jones, trying to focus. "I'm sorry could you repeat the question?" she asked softly.

The pastor smiled kindly. "Do you, Etta, take Cornelius Jr. Vanderbilt as your lawful husband?"

Etta swallowed, her voice barely a whisper. "I do." As she said it, her mind filled with questions. If he hadn't told her his real name, what else might he have hidden? Surely, the mail-order bride agency had known his true identity. Then a pang of guilt surfaced. She hadn't been completely honest with him either. Although she did write to Ester at the agency. But she didn't tell Cory that she had run from a powerful man back home, and that was no small secret. What would Cory think once he knew?

A weight settled in her heart, and she knew she couldn't keep her past hidden; it would feel too much like a lie. She would have to tell him, no matter how risky it felt. But now wasn't the time. With everything so new and her emotions raw, she needed a night's rest to process everything. Maybe after a good night's sleep, and some prayers, she'd be able to sort through the feeling, and find some clarity. Then she would tell him the truth with God's help.

Cory gently slid a ring on Etta's finger, its glimmer pulling her from her thoughts. She looked down, surprised by the delicate blue sapphire encircled by small, sparkling diamonds. It was breathtaking, catching the light in an almost magical way. Cory's fingers lingered on her, warm and steady, grounding her in the moment.

Etta lifted her gaze, meeting his eyes. For a moment, it was as if everything and everyone around them faded away.

Cory smiled softly, his voice low and sincere. "The sapphire isn't as beautiful as your blue eyes, but I thought of you the moment I saw it. Your picture didn't do you justice, and you wrote that you have blue eyes," he said, his gaze filled with warmth and admiration.

Etta's heart swelled, her surprise giving way to a deep sense of wonder and gratitude. She'd never expected something so thoughtful, so personal. For a moment she forgot every question, every worry about the future, and simply let herself feel the happiness in his words and the quiet strength in his touch. It had been a long time since she had been happy or even felt safe. She had prayed so hard for a good Christian, husband. Someone who would come to love her and that she could love. That they would have a good marriage not just one of convenience.

Pastor Jones interrupted the moment by saying, "You may kiss the bride."

Etta felt her heart flutter, barely able to catch her breath as Cory's gaze softened, a tender look in his eyes that made her feel as if she were the only person in the world. She barely had time to steady herself before he leaned in, his lips brushing hers in a gently, lingering kiss. A sweet warmth blossomed where his lips touched, and a spark of something new and thrilling coursed through her.

Then, as if sensing her hesitation melt into trust, Cory deepened the kiss ever so slightly. It wasn't rushed or intense, just full of quiet promises, a vow unspoken. For a moment, the worries, and fear from the past weeks fell away, and she was simply here with him, feeling his warmth, strength, and the hope, he held for their future together.

Just as quickly as it began, the kiss ended, leaving Etta breathless, her heart beating wildly. She blinked, feeling a bit dazed, but Cory's steady arms kept her grounded. He hadn't let go of her, his thumb tracing a gentle circle on her back as if to reassure her that this moment was real.

Cory hadn't meant to deepen the kiss, just intending a simple peck to seal their vows. But the moment his lips touched hers, a rush of emotions swept over him. It was a feeling he hadn't expected, powerful and deep. For a brief moment, he forgot everyone one else, lost in the softness and warmth of Etta's kiss. He felt a promise in that kiss, something tender yet strong, and his heart stirred with a longing he hadn't known until now.

Then, softly, he heard Malcom clear his throat, a gentle reminder that they weren't alone. Cory blinked, reality setting back in, but he didn't let go of Etta. He knew there were responsibilities and people waiting on him, tasks that couldn't be delayed. Yet, there was now a new urgency, a part of him that couldn't wait for the moment they'd finally be alone, able to talk to each other and maybe share another wonderful kiss. He wondered if the next kiss would be as good as the first one.

Paulette D. Marshall

Chapter Ten

The Ceremony

Pastor Jones hesitated to rush the newlyweds, but he knew time wasn't on their side. There was still so much to do, and with the sun inching lower, they'd soon be racing the setting light. He also knew his wife was probably worried, not knowing where he'd gone so suddenly. Clearing his throat gently, he said, "Before we head back, I'll need signatures on the marriage certificate. Luckily, I tucked it into my Bible earlier. Etta, Cory, Malcolm, and Miss Welsh, you'll all need to sign here."

Cory's attention was on Etta, his gaze filled with a blend of affection and protectiveness, but he noticed Miss Welsh had already gone to the wagon, likely after signing. Turning back to Etta, he watched her carefully sign her name, noting the slight tremble in her hand and the exhaustion etched into her face. He could feel an overwhelming need to care for her, protect her from whatever lay ahead. He wasn't expecting to feel that way. It took him by surprise.

After Malcom had signed, Cory took his turn with the pen, glancing up as Pastor Jones offered him a few last words. With the papers complete, Cory gently walked Etta to the wagon where he paused for a moment, taking one final look at the wreckage of the train. Wisps of smoke still rose from what remained of the engine, a haunting reminder of what had happened here. Metal was scattered everywhere signs of the blast that could have taken so many more lives. Quietly, he thanked God that it hadn't been worse. His heart hurt for all the lives that were changed today as he said a silent prayer for everyone.

Etta was determined to walk to the wagon by herself. Her legs felt like rubber. She just wanted to sit down and rest for a little bit. Maybe even close her eyes for a moment or two, but the thought of closing her eyes brought back images of today, and all the dead and injured. The images were still fresh in her mind. She had tried to pray with each of them, and if they didn't want to pray, she had prayed silently over them. She recognized the look in Cory's eyes, it was the same one he'd had earlier when he held her. A mixture of worry and determination, softened by a quiet tenderness. It was as if he were silently promising to protect her no matter the cost. That look spoke volumes, more than words ever could, and made her heart ache and swell at the same time.

Once seated in the wagon, Etta arranged her skirt. She wasn't even sure she could salvage her travel suit.

The Railroad Tycoon Rescue

With a firm grip on the reins, Cory flicked his wrist, setting the horses into motion. They moved steadily toward town, each mile bringing them closer to the new life they were beginning together.

The ride to town wasn't as long as it seemed like it took to get to the train, but with Etta sitting next to him he wished the ride was longer.

Etta enjoyed looking at the scenery. She tried to keep looking around so she wouldn't fall asleep. She didn't want to miss anything and soon could see the outline of the building miles away. Etta continued to watch, trying to absorb everything.

As they rode, she prayed for those who were injured and for those families that lost their loved ones.

"Will the families be notified of their loved ones who perished on the train?" Etta asked Cory.

"Yes, a telegram will be sent, and in some cases someone from the railroad will personally inform them of their loved one's demise," Cory answered.

"You seem to know a lot about it," Etta observed.

Cory nodded his head and then looked away.

Sitting next to Cory, she could feel the heat from him. They were sitting close, so their sides touched. Touching him sent tingles through her. She tried to distract herself by looking at the town they were approaching. She wanted to ask questions about the town and where his house was located. Even though they had written to each other, there was still so much she didn't know and there were things she needed to tell him. But it appeared everything would have to wait until later.

Cory started pointing out buildings and things as they passed the rail station. "There is a little Italian restaurant over there that is very good. It's owned by Rosebella and Lucas Corsello. Rosebella's sister is Annette who is married to our town sheriff, John."

As they drove by the Italian restaurant, the wonderful smell made Etta realize how hungry she was. It had been a long time since she last ate.

As they continued, he started pointing out more things, the courthouse, and mercantile. Unfortunately, there was also a two-story saloon and there was already music coming from it. The town didn't look large, but it was quaint, and it looked like it had everything one would need. She thought it was almost perfect, if only there wasn't a saloon. Cory even pointed out the church.

As he pulled the wagon to a stop in front of the hotel, he said, "I'm really sorry, but I need to do a few things in town before we head home. You can wait for me in the restaurant and have a cup of tea if you would like?"

The Railroad Tycoon Rescue

"I could use a cup of tea, but then I think I would like to check in with the doctor and see if they need any help. Where did you say the doctor's office is?" Etta asked as he dismounted.

"It's over there," he pointed, "but I think you have done enough for the day."

As Cory was waiting to help Etta down from the wagon, a man staggered up to him, clearly intoxicated. He shouted incoherently, slurring his words so much that most of it was garbled. Etta could make out only fragments, but one phrase struck her like a jolt: "Your train hurt a bunch of people…" The rest of his rambling was unintelligible, leaving her both shocked and puzzled. *What did he mean by "your train?"* Etta wanted to ask Cory, but before she could, the man wandered off, muttering to himself.

Cory gently guided her to the ground. She looked up at him, her brow furrowed. "What was that about?"

"Just Jack, the town drunk. He's harmless," Cory said dismissively, though his tone was a touch too quick. He offered a reassuring smile, but Etta couldn't shake the sense that there was more to this than he was letting on. She decided she'd learn more in time, though today didn't seem like the right moment to press him.

Just then, Malcolm and Pastor Jones approached Cory, and Etta took a step back to give them room to talk. She wandered a few paces away, gazing at the bustling town around her. She could still hear Cory, but his words were muffled. Curious, she turned to glance at him just as he spoke in a low voice.

"I'll take care of it. Thank you, Malcolm, for your advice and help. Tell Ester hi for me. We'll celebrate soon. She'll be glad to know," Cory said, his voice quiet but steady.

Etta's curiosity only grew. *Who was Ester?* She wondered if it could be the same Ester she knew from the mail-order bride agency. But "celebrate" what? She glanced at Cory, feeling the questions stacking up. In time, she silently thought, she'd find answers. For now, she'd have to wait and simply hope that this new life was one she could trust.

Cory walked up to her and led her into the hotel. They walked into the restaurant. He pulled the chair out for her. "Have whatever you like. I will be back as soon as I can. I'm sorry. This isn't how I pictured our day going. Just tell the waiter that you're Mrs. Vanderbilt and they can put it on my tab. I will also tell them at the front desk that my wife is in here," Cory said. As he turned a waitress came up to him. "This is my wife, serve her and put it on my tab."

Etta sat by the window, watching Cory walk away.

Cory walked to the train station first. Etta was lucky she could see most of the town from her seat. She ordered a cup of hot tea and water. She wasn't going to eat anything, hoping that they would be together for their first meal. Her stomach protested in a grumble. Etta had no idea how long Cory was going to be and prayed it wouldn't be too long. She was tired and hungry.

Stopping a waitress as she walked near her, she asked, "Can you tell me where the privy is?"

After washing her hands, she felt better. Sitting down at the table she wondered why she couldn't have gone with Cory. The waitress stopped and served her a small pot of tea, and set a plate with scones down next to it. "Thank you."

The waitress left and Etta poured herself a cup of tea. As she sipped, she looked out at the town. She watched Cory walk to the sheriff's office and noticed that everyone greeted him, and he seemed to be an important man in town. She wondered what he did. She didn't remember him mentioning what his job was. That would be one question she would have to ask him. The scones were delicious with her tea. She was feeling much better. Digging a nickel out of her purse, she sat it on the table and stood. The waitress came over to her. "Can I get you another pot of tea or something else?"

"No, thank you. That was perfect," Etta said.

"Have a good evening," the waitress said.

Etta walked outside and stood for a moment. Then she headed to the doctor's office. She was sure that they could still use her help.

Etta walked into the doctor's office. There were several people sitting waiting for the doctor and she recognized most of them. Doc Hendricks stepped out. "Etta, good to see you here. Are you having issues?"

"No, I'm fine, other than a slight headache. I thought you could use a little help?" Etta offered.

"If you have a headache still, I would like to check you over. You should be resting, not helping. I say you already helped enough," Doc Hendricks said with a smile.

"I'm fine, really. My husband had business to attend to, so I have a little time on my hands," Etta explained.

"Let me take a quick look at you first," Doc Hendricks said. Another doctor stepped into the room. "Doc Moor, may I introduce you to Etta. She helped at the accident. She has knowledge of herbs too. This is Doc Moor, the town doctor."

"Nice to meet you," Etta said.

"I was just going to check Etta out. Can I use your kitchen for a moment?" Doc Hendricks asked.

"That is fine. We seem to be pretty full. I want to move a couple of the less critical patients to the hotel if they have room. If not, I will have to figure something else out," Doc Moor said. "I need to get back to my patients." He scurried away.

"Please, humor me for just a moment, Etta," Doc Hendricks implored.

Etta gave in, "All right. But I'm telling you I'm fine."

Paulette D. Marshall

The Railroad Tycoon Rescue

Chapter Eleven

For Better or Worse

Doc Hendricks led her to a small but clean kitchen. He pulled a chair out for Etta, and she sat down. Doc Hendricks looked into her eyes, listened to her heart and felt her head. Etta winced but sat still.

Doc Hendricks gave her a kind but firm look. "I believe you're alright, but you need to rest and when was the last time you had a proper meal?" he asked, his tone gentle yet insistent.

Etta thought for a moment, trying to recall. "I had a lovely cup of tea and a scone before I headed over here," she replied with a smile. "I promise I'll eat and rest…but only after Cory returns." She realized she hadn't even asked him where their home was. If Cory didn't come back soon, she'd have to go to the hotel or ask if there was a boarding house, that she could stay in. She just hoped there was a room available, though she remembered hearing that everything was already full.

As she thought about Cory, her heart fluttered, her pulse quickening. He was more than handsome. There was a warmth to him, a strength that made her feel safe even in a town full of strangers. She couldn't quite put her finger on it, but something about him drew her in, made her want to know more.

But for now, her head was still hurting and all she could do was wait. She glanced at Doc Hendricks, who gave her an encouraging nod, as though he could sense her thoughts.

"I am here to help you in any way I can," Etta offered.

"We could use your help, but if you feel worse, I must insist that you sit and rest. It's a good thing there are two of us doctors here now," Doc Hendricks commented as they walked out of the kitchen together.

"Are you on your way to a different town?" Etta asked as she followed behind him.

"I am here to replace Doc Moor. He wants to retire," Doc Hendericks replied.

"God knew the town would need two doctors. At least for a time. Now, tell me what to do?" Etta asked.

Cory moved swiftly though town, focused on ensuring the injured were taken care of and their needs met. Determined to keep things organized, he had already visited the train station and requested a passenger list from the stationmaster. To streamline information, he appointed the stationmaster to gather the names of the injured so they could identify everyone, especially those who had not survived. He also arranged for the train to come from the nearest town to pick up the few passengers that needed to travel onward that were able to travel.

His next stop was the undertakers to arrange dignified burials for those who perished. The weight of the tragedy pressed heavily on him; he knew this accident had come at a great cost, both in terms of life and resources. But he wasn't just willing to cover their immediate needs. Cory felt a deep obligation to ensure this never happened again, or at least to minimize the risks. He made a mental note to find out what had gone wrong with the train and explore what could be done to prevent similar tragedies in the future.

As he walked back through town, his shoulders were squared, and his steps deliberate, each one carrying the weight of his responsibility. His jaw was set, and his gaze fixed ahead, barely acknowledging the people who stopped to watch him pass. There was no hesitation in his stride, only the determination of a man who knew others were counting on him. His heart ached for the lives that were lost, but his resolve was steadfast. He wouldn't let this pass without seeking answers and ensuring the community was safe.

His last stop for the day would be to pay for the passengers that were staying at the boarding house and a few at the hotel. After a quick stop earlier at the mercantile, he'd arranged to cover all the essentials that they'd need during their recovery.

Cory quietly prayed as he made his way to the boarding house, hoping the consequences from the accident wouldn't be as severe as Malcom had warned him. Malcom was a lawyer and had dealt with more than he had but Cory knew that legal troubles could not only drain him financially but also tarnish the reputation of his family and the railroad.

He sighed, thinking of the lives lost and the ones suffering. "Please, Lord," he whispered, "help me handle whatever comes next."

But his prayers weren't just for the injured or for financial protection. His thoughts turned to Etta. He prayed that her injury would heal swiftly, and that she wouldn't suffer any lasting effects. She was still so new to his life, and he was still coming to terms with the fact that she was his wife. As he thought of her, his heart softened with a mixture of gratitude and nervousness. This was not how he imagined their first days of marriage. He had hoped to show her the town under different, happier circumstances and to settle into their life together with ease.

Yet, despite the rough beginning, he felt a sense of peace about their union. Etta was an extremely beautiful woman. He couldn't believe she wasn't already married. Perhaps it was all God's hand at work, bringing them together in the middle of turmoil, forcing them to rely on one another sooner than they'd planned. He prayed that they would both find strength in each other as they started their marriage and that they could face whatever came their way together.

Cory carried a small package. He had picked up a few things for Etta when he was at the mercantile. As he had passed the soaps, there was one that reminded him of her. He had smelled a faint rose smell. He picked it up, and some hair pins, combs, and a hair ribbon that was the same color blue as her eyes. He wasn't sure what else she would need; he would just have to bring her back tomorrow.

As Cory walked by the window of the restaurant in the hotel and looked in, he didn't see Etta inside. Maybe he missed her because she was in the privy. After he took care of his business, he took one last look for Etta. Not finding her, he asked the desk clerk, who said "Mrs. Vanderbilt said she was going over to Doc's."

"Thank you," Cory said. He walked to the boarding house. He was glad to know that his wife had been caring and attentive to others in need.

Cory's own exhaustion had begun to weigh on him. He was ready to go home, and he hoped that Etta was too. He knew she had to be exhausted. More than anything, he wanted time alone with his wife. He never imagined he'd feel so drawn to her this quickly.

When he walked into the doctor's office, he noticed the waiting room was empty, but he could hear voices from the back. Doc Hendricks came out with a tired but friendly smile.

"Good evening. Your wife has been an incredible help. But I'm glad you're here to take her home," Doc Hendricks said.

"I'm grateful she was able to help, but I think it's time for her to rest. Is she ready to leave?" Cory asked, glancing down the hall. "I will take care of the bill for those injured from the train."

Doc Henricks nodded. "I'll go get her. And thank you for taking care of the medical bills for the injured passengers. It's a generous gesture."

Cory nodded. "It's only right," he said. "If there's anything else they need, let me know."

A moment later, Etta appeared, looking tired but relieved. She caught the tail end of their conversation, and was surprised to hear Cory was paying for all the medical expenses. Why would he take on such a burden?

The Railroad Tycoon Rescue

Cory's gaze softened as he looked at him. "Are you ready to go home?" he asked gently, holding out his hand.

"Yes," Etta replied, taking his hand. As they walked out, she couldn't shake her curiosity. Cory seemed to be carrying a weight she didn't fully understand. But for now, she was grateful to have him by her side, and to finally leave the long, exhausting day behind.

After Cory helped her into the wagon, he gave her his little gift.

Etta carefully unwrapped the brown paper to reveal an assortment of treasures, hairpins, ribbon, combs, and wonderfully fragrant soap that smelled of roses with a hint of lavender. She picked up the combs, admiring the intricate design inlaid with delicate pearls.

"These combs are exquisite, and it was so thoughtful to get me more hair pins. Thank you, Cory," she said, her voice soft with gratitude. The gift was not only beautiful but thoughtful. She had lost most of her hair pins in the accident, and now with these in hand she felt a touch of normalcy returning.

Sitting close to Cory sent pleasant tingles through Etta. She wanted to lean into him, to rest her head on his shoulder, but she held back unsure of how he might react or how long their journey would take. The wagon ride gave her a perfect view of the surroundings as they passed through town. When Cory turned down a long lane, Etta's eyes widened as she saw their destination.

The house, or maybe she should call it a mansion, loomed in the fading light, elegant and grand, with columns and a wrap around porch. Her mouth fell open in shock. This was far more than she'd ever imagined. She glanced over at Cory, unable to hide her surprise.

Cory met her gaze, his expression soft but serious. "I didn't lie, but I did leave out a couple of things. I never had a chance to explain," he began, his voice low, almost pleading. "I wanted to talk before our wedding, but fate has had other plans. I'm hoping that you will give me a chance to be open and honest with you. I know there is a lot to take in, and I hope you will allow me the chance to share everything with you."

Etta took a breath, steading herself. "I would like that very much, Cory," she replied, her voice calm and filled with sincerity. "I believe in honesty, and it seems there are a few things we both left unsaid. I hope we'll have time to talk, to understand each other."

Cory reached over, gently taking her hand, and nodded. "We'll have that time, Etta. I promise."

The Railroad Tycoon Rescue

At the mansion, a warm light glowed from within. It looked welcoming and despite everything that was still unsaid, Etta's heart swelled with hope that this place and this man were her home now.

Cory guided the wagon to a stop in front of the grand house. Almost immediately, the front door opened, and an older woman stepped outside, her posture poised and commanding. Following closely behind her was a man in a crisp uniform, his demeanor formal and professional. Etta guessed he was the butler, the way he stood at attention, his hands clasped neatly behind his back, left little doubt.

"Cory, I was getting worried. I am so glad you're home," the lady said, her voice tinged with concern and relief.

Cory dismounted and held his hand to help Etta down. "Grandmother, I'm sorry it took us so long. There was a train accident, and I had to see to things," he explained as Etta stepped onto the ground. Once she was steady, he gestured between them. "Grandmother, I would like to introduce my wife, Etta. Etta, this is my grandmother, Beatrice." He led her closer, his tone warm.

Etta offered a polite smile, wishing she'd had a chance to freshen up before this introduction, but it wasn't meant to be. "It's nice to meet you," she said with a small smile, her voice steady despite her nerves.

Beatrice smiled warmly, her eyes filled with curiosity and kindness. "It's very nice to meet you, my dear. You may call me either Beatrice or Grandmother, whichever feels right to you. Thank goodness you've arrived safely, Etta."

Etta returned the sincere smile, dipping her head slightly in understanding. "Thank you, Grandmother," she said softly, already feeling a sense of welcome despite the unexpected circumstances.

Grandmother continued, "Cory, I look forward to hearing more about the accident whenever you have a chance. Etta, I'm sure that you are tired after your journey, dear. Cory can show you to your room. I look forward to chatting with you tomorrow. I already ate, so you two can have some time alone together. Good night."

"Good night, Grandmother," Cory said as they walked inside the house with his arm around his wife's waist.

The entryway stretched out before her, grand and imposing, with soaring ceilings and a staircase that swept gracefully to the upper floors. The staircase hinted at a house of three levels, each promising its own kind of elegance and charm. The polished oak railing gleamed under the soft light, its rich wood glowing with a warmth that spoke of care and refinement.

Etta couldn't help but marvel at the opulence surrounding her. It had been years since she'd been in a home this elegant. Her parents' house had once been refined, though it couldn't compare to the splendor of this place. Glimpses of beauty caught her eye, paintings hung on the walls, intricate moldings adorning the ceilings, and stately furniture that exuded quiet sophistication. Much of the house remained hidden from view, but what she saw was enough to take her breath away.

Cory gently led her up the staircase, his hand light on the small of her back, guiding her with ease. As they reached the second floor, they walked down a wide hallway lined with finely painted portraits. The faces in the paintings seemed to watch them pass, and Etta wondered if they were family members, each with a story of their own. She couldn't wait to learn more about them.

They stopped in front of a heavy wooden door. Cory opened it with a soft creak and stepped aside to let her in. The room was spacious with a high ceiling, and warm. A large fireplace flickered softly on one wall, casting a cozy glow across the room. There were comfortable chairs arranged around a small table, with a bookshelf stacked high with books. Etta noticed a large bed along one wall, draped with rich, soft linens that invited rest.

Cory's voice was gentle as he spoke. "There's a privy inside, so you won't have to go outside. I thought you'd appreciate that." His eyes held a hint of concern, as though he wanted to make sure everything was to her liking.

Etta stood in the doorway for a moment, taking it all in. It was far more than she expected. "This is beautiful," she whispered, feeling both grateful and slightly overwhelmed. She noticed her carpet bag was sitting on top of her steam trunk.

"My luggage. How did you manage that?" Etta was surprised and grateful to see them. She thought it would take days to get them back.

"I will explain everything while we eat. Did you want to freshen up first?" Cory asked her.

"Yes, please. If you don't mind?" Etta asked.

"Take your time," Cory encouraged. That would give him time to wash up too.

Etta headed to the privy, grateful for a moment to herself. A sense of peace washed over her. Yet, beneath that calm, the weight of the truth she needed to reveal pressed heavily on her, stirring a nervous flutter in her chest.

The Railroad Tycoon Rescue

Chapter Twelve

Truth or Excuse

Etta stepped into the room, her eyes widening. A table before the fireplace was set with a variety of delicious looking food, Bread, roasted meat, cheeses, and fresh fruit, were all arranged with care. A single candle flickered at the center of the spread, casting a warm glow over the meal. She couldn't remember the last time she'd seen such a feast, not since before her parents had passed. Her mouth watered and her stomach grumbled softly in anticipation.

Cory was standing by one of the tall windows, his gaze distant, and he looked out into the evening light. Hearing her enter, he turned, a warm smile lighting up his face. He took in her expression, clearly noticing her wonder at the simple yet thoughtful gesture. He wanted to keep that smile on her face; it was such a treasure.

"I thought we might enjoy our meal here so that we can talk privately," he said, gesturing to the table. "I wasn't sure what you'd like, so I had them prepare a little bit of everything."

Paulette D. Marshall

Etta felt a wave of gratitude rise in her chest, mingling with an unexpected shyness. The quiet meal, with just the two of them, felt more intimate than she had anticipated. It was as if this was his way of welcoming her into his life. This was far more than what she was expecting. She thought she would be making the meal this evening.

"It's perfect," she said, her voice catching just slightly. "I…I don't remember the last time I had a meal like this."

Cory walked over to her, holding out a chair for her to sit. "Then let's make sure it's one you'll remember." He pushed her chair in and sat down next to her. "I would like to say a prayer before we eat, if you don't mind?"

"I'd love that," Etta softly replied, bowing her head as Cory said grace. After grace was finished, Cory started dishing up the food, making sure that Etta put some on her plate too. They started eating.

After a few moments of silence, Cory took a deep breath and said, "I'm sorry I left some things out of my letter. I had my reasons."

Etta looked at him thoughtfully, dabbing her mouth with a linen napkin. "I'm sure you did," she replied softly. "My parents had money, too. Nothing as grand as this, of course, but I know how wealth can complicate things. I can imagine why you might not have mentioned it."

The Railroad Tycoon Rescue

Cory nodded, then stood and reached for her hand, helping her from the chair. He let her over to a cozy loveseat near the fireplace, where they sat close together. With his arm resting along the back of the seat, he looked at her earnestly, the firelight casting a warm glow over her face.

"When people realize you have money," he began, his voice low, "it changes things. For some, it's all they see. They don't see you as a person anymore. All they see is wealth. I don't want that. I wanted someone who wanted me, not my fortune."

Etta felt her heart soften as he spoke. She could see he was opening up, revealing a part of himself he rarely shared. In that moment, she caught a glimpse of the real Cory, a man who longed to be seen and loved for who he was. She felt drawn to him, a connection growing between them that surprised her with its depth.

Cory leaned a little closer, his gaze never leaving hers. Slowly, he brought his lips to hers in a tender kiss, filled with both warmth and a hint of a promise of their new beginning. The kiss was gentle yet full of longing, carrying the weight of all the words he hadn't said.

As they drew apart, Etta's heart was racing, her breath a little unsteady. She met his gaze, and for the first time, she truly felt like she belonged right here with him. But she knew she should also share with Cory about Mr. Warren. She was praying that he wouldn't follow her and make trouble.

"Etta, I want a real marriage, in every way. If you want a little time to get to know each other, I am willing to wait, although I would prefer not."

Etta was silent for a moment. She expected the same. After all, she pledged before God. "We are married, and I would like a real marriage," she whispered.

The next morning Etta woke up by herself. After dressing, she wandered down the stairs, not quite sure of where she was going. She found the parlor and walked though it to the dining room. What a relief to find it. There was a massive dining table that was set with China and crystal glasses. There was fine art all around, and a fancy sideboard that had silver pans with candles underneath them. The walls were covered with elaborate wallpaper and every surface held porcelain, silver, and glass.

Etta walked to the side table. Lifting the lid off one of the silver pans, she discovered scrambled eggs nestled inside. She lifted another lid and there were pieces of sliced ham. One held biscuits and another held gravy.

"Ma'am, we kept breakfast warm for you. May I assist you in any way?" the butler asked.

"No, thank you. This all smells delicious," she said as she picked up a China plate and selected her choices for breakfast.

The Railroad Tycoon Rescue

"Good morning," Cory said as he walked up behind her and put his hand on her back as he leaned around and kissed her.

"Good morning. I'm sorry I slept so late," Etta said, a touch of embarrassment in her voice.

Cory gave her an understanding smile. "You were tired after all that traveling. It's completely understandable"

"Sir, may I help you?" the butler inquired.

"No, thank you, Mr. Hargrove. That will be all for the moment," Cory said and gently dismissed the butler as he picked up a coffee cup and poured coffee into it.

"Very good, sir. Ring if you need anything," Mr. Hargrove said before he walked out of the room.

They sat down close together. "You never told me what job you have, if any. Although I might be able to guess since I learned your birth name," Etta said.

"If your guess was a railroad baron, you would have been correct. I do have an office in town and one here. If you have time after you finish eating, I can give you a tour of the house," Cory offered with a smile as he drank his coffee.

Etta smiled at her husband and replied, "I would love that."

Paulette D. Marshall

A week had passed as Etta began adjusting to her new life. Grandmother had decided that Etta should take charge of running the house, since she turned the house over to her and Cory, although she was always ready to guide her or offer suggestions when needed.

Managing a large household was nothing new to Etta, though it had been some time since she'd done so. The routines and responsibilities were familiar, and she quickly found herself settling into the role with confidence.

They even had a piano, a beautiful instrument that was positioned by a big window and it immediately caught Etta's attention. It had been so long since she'd played, and her fingers itched to touch the keys. Selling her piano had been one of the hardest decisions she'd ever made, a loss that still lingered in her heart.

At first, she wondered if she should ask for permission before playing, but one quiet afternoon, the temptation proved too strong. Sitting down on the bench, she let her hand glide over the smooth ivory keys, savoring the feel of the instrument. The piano was exquisite, its polished surface gleaming in the soft light.

Tentatively, she pressed a single note. The rich sound filled the air, awakening a deep longing within her. One note led to another, and soon she was playing her favorite songs, the music flowing effortlessly. She became so absorbed in the melody that she didn't even notice when Cory walked into the room, his presence as quiet as the shadows.

When the last note of the song faded, Etta kept her hands resting on the piano keys, her eyes closed, savoring the moment.

Cory stood behind her, watching with admiration. "That was beautiful," he murmured softly, hating to break the spell she wove with the music. "I didn't know you could play the piano."

Etta opened her eyes and looked up at him, a hint of homesickness in her gaze. "Yes, I do. As I'd mentioned before, my mother raised me to be a proper southern belle. I learned piano, painting, embroidery, and how to run a household. Among other things," she replied, her voice carrying a blend of pride and sorrow. "But in the hard years after she and my father passed, none of those skills or talents, mattered much. There was no call for piano or paintings, just the need to work hard."

Cory placed a gentle kiss on her cheek, his heart aching for what she had endured. "I'm sorry, my dear. I wish I could have been there to help. But sometimes, God has us walk through the fire to refine us." He squeezed her shoulder, marveling at how much closer they'd grown over the past week.

He cleared his throat, adding, "The railroad investigator is in town. I thought we could invite him for dinner tonight if that's all right with you darling." Cory couldn't deny it any longer, he was falling deeply in love with his wife. She was graceful, poised, and intelligent, yet unafraid of hard work. He could tell she'd gone without many comforts; her hands were rough, and she was slender from lean times. But she didn't mind getting her hands dirty. Just yesterday, she had cleared some weeds from the garden without hesitation. And, after some gentle nudging from him and a few suggestions from his grandmother, Etta had finally agreed to allow the dressmaker to visit the house and set up a new wardrobe.

"That sounds nice and I'm sure the railroad investigator will give you his report soon," Etta replied, a soft smile lighting her face. "I'll go let Cook know we'll have one more at the table tonight and I will tell your grandmother too."

Cory held up a hand. "Wait a moment," he said gently. "I wanted to give you a heads-up that he might have questions for you. He's been speaking with everyone still in town who was on the train."

Etta nodded, though a flicker of apprehension crossed her face. "I'd rather not revisit that incident, but I'll do my best to answer whatever questions he might have."

Cory watched her leave the room, concern deepening in his gaze. He only hoped talking about the accident wouldn't trigger more nightmares. She'd had a few already, and each time he saw her struggling with the memories, his heart broke a little more. He vowed to do

The Railroad Tycoon Rescue

whatever he could to help her heal, standing by her side through every hardship.

Cory had already invited Malcom and Ester for dinner, which was a good addition now that the investigator was joining them as well. Having Malcom, an attorney, at the table would lend a layer of protection if things got tense or too probing. His grandmother would, of course, also be present. Since she lived with them, she was part of every gathering, bringing warmth and charm that kept the household lively. Fortunately, her personal wing in the house allowed Cory and Etta the privacy they needed as newlyweds, but he was thankful that his grandmother and Etta were already forming a close bond. They seemed to genuinely enjoy each other's company, filling the house with natural warmth and camaraderie he hadn't fully anticipated.

Etta was eager to finally meet Ester in person. From the letter she had received from her, it sounded like they'd get along well, and she hoped they might even become friends. Especially since Cory was Ester's cousin and he was friends with Malcom. Moving to a new town had been a whirlwind, and she hadn't had much of a chance to form too many female connections outside the house. The few people she'd met had been kind, but building real friendships took time, and she missed that sense of companionship.

Despite her eagerness, a faint thread of worry tugged at her. She still had spells of dizziness that seemed to come out of nowhere, leaving her feeling lightheaded. Doc Hendricks had reassured her that these were likely a lingering effect from the accident, combined with the toll of long-term malnutrition before arriving here. Doc seemed to think that with good food and rest she would be her old self in no time. Cory had encouraged her to rest and not push herself, and Etta knew he was right, but it was frustrating not being fully herself. Meeting new people tonight, however, gave her something to look forward to.

Before the guests arrived, Etta, dressed in one of her new dresses, was checking over the table one last time. Cory came into the room. "Here you are, darling. Come sit in the front room with me and Grandmother. Everything looks and smells wonderful. I am sure our servants have everything under control."

"I know you're right, but I just wanted one last look. You look very handsome," Etta said with a smile.

"I know you're nervous about tonight and the questions the investigator is going to ask. But I won't leave you alone. You will be fine," Cory tried to reassure her.

Etta looked into her handsome husband's warm, steady gaze; her own eyes filled with worry. "I am nervous about it," she admitted, "but more than that, I'm worried about you and your railroad. Do you think they're going to hold you responsible?"

The Railroad Tycoon Rescue

Chapter Thirteen

Secrets

Etta's voice was soft, but her concern was clear. She reached out, placing a gentle hand on his arm, as though trying to protect him from the weight of it all. She searched his face, hoping for a reassurance but also prepared to stand by him no matter what.

"Darling," Cory said, his voice warm and steady, "no matter what happens, as long as we have each other and God in our lives, we're the richest people in the world. Family is what truly matters. We can always start over if we have to, because money isn't everything." He looked at her with a deep sense of gratitude, recognizing how blessed he was to have her in his life.

Cory wanted to tell her he loved her, but he knew their guests would be arriving at any moment. Instead, he took her gently in his arms, giving her a kiss that held all the feelings he hadn't yet put into words. He never realized that he could fall in love so quickly, but he did. Feeling truly fortunate, he placed a hand on the small of her back and led her toward the front room.

The kiss Cory gave her sent tingles through her as she melted in her husband's arms. The kiss relaxed her more than the words he had spoken. She knew what ever happened they would survive.

"You look especially beautiful tonight. Is this one of your new dresses?" Cory asked softly, admiring her.

"Yes, it is. Do you like it?" Etta asked, her cheeks tinged with a soft blush.

"It brings out the color of your blue eyes," he whispered, leaning close, "and I wish we were alone so I could properly tell you just how lovely you are."

Etta giggled, just as Beatrice cleared her throat in a subtle reminder that she was in the room.

"Sorry, Grandmother," Cory said with a smile. Etta blushed as he led her to the loveseat, where she sat gracefully. Smiling, he asked, "Would you care or anything to drink, darling?"

"I would love a glass of water, please," Etta replied.

"Grandmother, would you care for anything to drink?" Cory asked.

"I would love some lemonade," Grandmother answered.

The Railroad Tycoon Rescue

After Cory handed out the drinks, he sat next to Etta. It wasn't long before Ester and Malcom arrived.

Etta was thrilled to finally meet Ester. They formed an instant connection, and she already felt as though Ester could become a dear friend.

Just behind them, Inspector Birdwhistle entered the room.

Cory stepped forward, saying, "I'd like to introduce Inspector Birdwhistle. Inspector, this is my lovely wife, Etta, and my grandmother, Beatrice. I believe you already know Malcom and his wife, Ester."

"Pleased to meet you, Mrs. Vanderbilt," Inspector Birdwhistle greeted with a courteous nod. He turned to Etta. "Mrs. Vanderbilt, I hope it would be ok to call you Etta? It might get confusing if I called you both Mrs. Vanderbilt."

"That would be fine," Etta replied.

Inspector Birdwhistle continued, "It's a pleasure to meet you at last. Mrs. Davis and Malcom, good to see you again."

The butler approached, bowing slightly. "May I offer you a drink, Inspector?"

"Yes, thank you, a glass of water would be lovely," Inspector Birdwhistle replied.

The inspector settled into a chair, and the group enjoyed light conversation until the butler returned, announcing "Dinner is served."

Once seated, Cory said, "I would like to say a prayer before we eat."

After dinner, Inspector Birdwhistle turned to Etta with a gentle but serious expression. "Etta, I hope we might take a few minutes to go over the accident. I'd like to hear directly from you, if that is alright."

Etta felt a wave of discomfort wash over her. She hadn't wanted to relive that day. But she knew if she held back, the inspector might assume she was hiding something or trying to protect Cory. Back then, she didn't know he was the owner of the train. Saying a silent prayer for guidance before taking a deep breath, she began recounting the tragic event.

"The train ride felt so normal at first," she said, her voice quiet but steady. "Everyone was talking, smiling, and enjoying the trip. Then all of a sudden, the train started swaying, gently at first but growing worse. I didn't think too much of it until there was a deafening crunch, like metal being torn apart. A terrible screech echoed through the railcar. It's hard to describe, but… it felt endless. Then people were screaming, crying, calling for help. I remember opening my eyes and finding myself on what I thought was the floor of the railcar, but it was the side of the railcar, surrounded by broken glass and shattered wood."

The Railroad Tycoon Rescue

Etta's face had grown pale, and she seemed to struggle to continue. Even though she had helped many people with tonics and herbal medication, this was very different. There was so much blood, and mangled people who needed more help than she could give, especially without her herbs at the accident, which made her feel so helpless. She had prayed with many of them, but somehow it felt like she hadn't done enough. She even felt guilty for not being hurt worse. Oh, she had bruises and bumps, but people had lost their lives… Shaking her head, she tried to clear those thoughts as she silently prayed for those still healing and for God's guidance and forgiveness.

Cory tightened his arm around Etta, drawing her close in a protective embrace. He turned to the inspector, his voice firm but respectful. "Inspector, I think that's enough. Etta has relived this ordeal more than she should have to. She helped many of the injured. She's been struggling with nightmares as it is."

"The information that Etta provided is more than enough," Inspector Birdwhistle said, nodding with appreciation. "Her account aligns closely with what other passengers have described."

He turned to Cory, his tone both professional and reassuring. "I should have the final report ready and on your desk tomorrow or the next day."

Cory let out a subtle sigh of relief, thankful that Etta wouldn't have to endure more questions, and he would soon have some answers. He gave her hand a gentle squeeze, and she managed a small, grateful smile in return. He just wanted to protect his beautiful bride.

Cory looked at her. "Etta, would you honor us with some music? Etta is a wonderful piano player, and I enjoy her music when she graces me with it."

"I would be honored to play for you," Etta said as she sat down and started to play. The tension from re-living the accident was slowly starting to drain away. Music always relaxed her, and she loved to play.

A loud knock sounded at the front door, making everyone glance up. Etta, seated at the piano, continued to play, filling the room with warm, soothing notes. The guests smiled and relaxed in their seats, enjoying the music.

Raised voices could be heard coming from the entryway, followed by a loud thud and a harsh shout which disturbed the music and the peace. Everyone fell silent, and Cory rose from his chair, his gaze fixed on the hall as he moved to investigate the disturbance. Just before he reached the doorway, a man appeared, stepping into the room unannounced and it wasn't the butler, but a stranger to him.

Etta's fingers continued on the keys for a moment before she looked up. The movement at the door had caught her attention. A man stood there in a suit, but when her eyes rose to his face her playing slowed. When her eyes met the man's furious, flushed face, she froze. Her heart plummeted, and all the color drained from her cheeks. She knew that face.

It couldn't be, yet here he was, standing in her new home, the look of rage unmistakable in his mean, cruel eyes.

Paulette D. Marshall

The Railroad Tycoon Rescue

Chapter Fourteen

Secrets Revealed

This couldn't be happening. Etta blinked, hoping he'd disappear, but he was still standing in her home, his presence heavy and suffocating. She'd prayed she'd left him far behind. How had he found her? How had he gotten here so quickly, and did this mean the train line was restored?

"There you are. I demand that you come home now!" he bellowed, his face flushed crimson, his cruel, unyielding eyes fixed on her with a look of possession that sent a chill down her spine.

Etta felt paralyzed, her voice lost somewhere between her throat and her pounding heart.

Cory stepped forward, his expression darkening. "Who are you, and what do you think you're doing, barging into my home like this?" His voice was calm but commanding as he stood to the side of the intruder, ready to intervene or move to block him.

Cory's gaze flicked to Etta, and in that moment, he saw her fear. A fear and terror he'd never seen in her before. Realization dawned; something was horribly wrong. He turned his head slightly, calling, "Hargrove, where are you?"

Across the room, Malcom rose from his chair, sensing the tension thickening like a storm in the air. His eyes settled on Etta, catching the unmistakable terror etched across her face. This wasn't just any stranger. This was something or someone from Etta's past.

Every instinct Etta had screamed for her to run, but she was frozen, fear gripping her like an iron shackle. All she could do was whisper a silent plea: Please, God help me.

Ester rushed to Etta's side, her hand resting gently on her arm. "Etta, are you ok?" she whispered, her voice soft but urgent.

Etta blinked, her lips parting, but no words would come.

"What is wrong?" Ester whispered again, a note of alarm in her voice. "You have to tell me so I can help." She had an inkling of what might be happening, especially after reading Etta's recent letter.

Suddenly, the man bellowed. "I'm here to take my wife back!"

A stunned silence fell over the room.

Etta's chest tightened as his words sank in. *Wife?* She wasn't his wife, and she'd never agreed to marry him. Only a desperate woman would let herself be trapped by that brute. It would be a death sentence. His bullying and manipulation had nearly destroyed her once; she wasn't going back.

Cory stepped forward, blocking the stranger's path. "I don't know what you're talking about, but get out of my home, or I'll call the sheriff."

The man's sneer deepened. "The sheriff shouldn't be too far behind me. I went to him first, but he tried to tell me that my betrothed had already married another. So, I looked at the certificate on file and it's not legal," he said, his gaze boring into Etta with venom.

Etta's voice found its strength, and she stood up, chin raised. "I am not your betrothed, nor did I agree to marry you. How dare you barge in here and slander my name!" She would not let this man terrorize her again. Everyone back home already wondered what happened to his first wife. There were rumors that she tried to leave and hadn't succeeded. Etta's face was set in defiance. She would not be another one of his victims.

The sheriff entered the room, supporting Hargrove, who leaned on him, wincing in pain. "Sorry, sir. He slugged me when I wouldn't let him in," Hargrove said as the sheriff helped him sit down in a nearby chair.

Etta rushed over to Hargrove, pulling out her handkerchief to gently dab at the blood on his face. Her eyes flashed. "You ought to be ashamed of yourself, Mr. Warren, for hurting this man who was only doing his job," she scolded sharply. Then, her expression softened as she turned back to Hargrove. "We need to get Doc Moor or Doc Hendricks to check him over."

One of the maids, sensing the urgency, scurried away to fetch the doctor.

The sheriff straightened, his gaze steely as he turned to Warren. "Mr. Warren, I think it is best if you come with me. I am sure we'll get everything straightened out in time, but you've just forced your way into another man's home and assaulted an innocent man. It's best you cool off in jail for the night. I told you I'd look into this, and I will, but not like this."

Warren's eyes narrowed as he puffed up his chest, undeterred. "Now see here, Sheriff! I have every right to retrieve my wayward woman," he insisted, voice booming with indignation.

Etta felt a shiver run down her spine, but she stood her ground. Raising her chin, she met Warren's gaze, refusing to be cowed. "I am not your wayward woman, Mr. Warren," she said firmly. "I never agreed to marry you. You may have taken my house, but you never had any claim to me. I'd been writing to Cory for months before I left. I never intended to marry you, no matter how you've tried to force me." She paused, her voice trembling with strength and emotion. "And I will not end up like your first wife, Sherry."

The Railroad Tycoon Rescue

The room fell into a heavy silence. Everyone's gaze darted between Etta and Mr. Warren, absorbing everything they had heard. Mr. Warren's face flushed an even deeper red. His fist clenched, but the sheriff's firm hand on his shoulder prevented him from moving any closer.

Cory stepped to Etta's side, placing a reassuring hand on her shoulder. "Mr. Warren," he said, voice calm but edged with steel, "you will respect my wife's wishes and this household. She is no longer alone."

"How do I know that this man isn't holding her against her will?" Mr. Warren demanded.

"I can vouch for Cory. He would never do anything like that. He is an upstanding citizen, and he lives with his grandmother," Sheriff John stated.

There was another knock on the door as sheriff John was leaving with Mr. Warren.

A man walked into the room.

"George. Good to see you," Cory said, even though this wasn't the time for one of his lawyers to show up. Or maybe it was. He could help with this mess. Cory wanted time alone to talk to Etta.

Etta watched as the grounds keeper helped Hargrove out of the room and to his room.

"I think it's past time for me to leave. Thank you for a pleasant dinner and for talking to me, Etta and Cory. Good evening," Inspector

Birdwhistle said as he shook Cory's hand. "I will have that report to you as soon as possible."

"Thank you and sorry about our interruption," Cory offered.

"It wasn't your fault. Good night," Inspector Birdwhistle said before he left.

"George, while it is always good to see you, I have a feeling that I'm not going to like whatever you have to say," Cory said to his lawyer. "Would you like to sit down?"

"I suggest we go into your office and talk," George said. "Maybe Malcom should join us and your wife."

Cory turned to his grandmother, "Grandmother, Ester, if you will excuse us," Cory said as he kissed her cheek. "I will get to the bottom of what happened here and about the marriage, not to mention his claim on Etta. Once I know everything, I will share it with you."

"Wait, what was that you are saying?" George asked.

Cory looked at George and felt dread. "That man stormed in and claimed that Etta was his intended. Then he spouted something to the effect that we weren't legally married," Cory scoffed as he looked at George. He noticed that George's face was grim. What had started out as a wonderful evening was turning into something tragic. They were so happy earlier. Cory silently

The Railroad Tycoon Rescue
whispered a prayer, *"Lord, I could use your help and protection."*

"I think we all need to sit and pray for a moment. Whatever is coming our way, we need to stand as a family," Ester advised. Everyone sat down. Cory sat next to Etta.

"I couldn't agree more," Grandmother said.

"I will pray," Malcom said as everyone bowed their heads. "Lord, we need you to guide and protect this family. Show us your way and the truth. Amen."

Cory looked at George and said, "George, I think whatever you came to say to me, that you should just share."

"I hate to be the bearer of bad news, but what that man said was correct. The marriage isn't legal and your deadline for the inheritance is tomorrow. If you aren't legally married by tomorrow, you will lose the company," George revealed.

"What? That's ridiculous. Pastor Jones married us. It has to be legal," Cory stated with a little bit of anger and desperation. Cory ran his hand through his hair. This couldn't be happening. That would mean that he and Etta were living in sin since they weren't legally married.

"That part is legal, but there is a signature that is missing," George tried to explain.

"I was there and one of the witnesses. I signed. Let me please see that certificate," Malcom asked.

George handed over the certificate. Cory leaned over to look at it too. "That can't be right. I saw Mrs. Miller pick up the pen."

"But there isn't a signature there," George said as he pointed out the blank spot.

"Something must have happened and she didn't get the chance to sign it," Malcom said.

"I guess I was a little preoccupied," Cory said as he looked at his lovely wife.

Etta stood in shock, trying to piece together what was being said about the will. The words swirled in her mind, and something about not being married and living in sin made her stomach twist. It couldn't be true, could it?

Cory must have noticed her distress. He held up a hand to the men. "Just a moment. I need to speak with Etta." Turning to her, his voice softened. "Darling, I told you I didn't want anyone to know about our family money. But what I didn't get a chance to explain was this: there's a clause in my grandfather's will. It requires me to be married before my twenty-third birthday to secure the inheritance."

He stepped closer, his gaze steady and full of sincerity. "But listen to me. None of that matters as much as you do. You're more important to me than my family's company. I love you, Etta."

The Railroad Tycoon Rescue

Etta gazed into Cory's eyes, and saw deep, unwavering love reflected back at her. Her heart swelled with emotion. "I love you too, Cory," she said softly, her voice trembling slightly.

She hesitated, then continued, her expression tinged with regret. "I'm sorry I didn't get a chance to tell you about Mr. Warren. It was never my intention to keep it a secret. I truly believe that if I left and he got the house, he'd be happy and move on…maybe even find someone else. I guess I was wrong."

"A greedy man like that won't give easily," Cory said, his tone steady but understanding. "I get it, Etta. We've been busy getting better to know each other, and there hasn't been much time to share everything. But as we move forward, I hope we can be more open and honest with each other."

"I couldn't agree with you more," Etta said as Cory bent over and kissed her.

While they were talking the others were sharing ideas on how to clear this all up.

Malcom cleared his throat. He said, "If you two have a few minutes. I believe we have figured out how to fix this issue."

Paulette D. Marshall

The Railroad Tycoon Rescue

Chapter Fifteen

Joining Two Hearts

"I believe we can fix this issue tonight. I will start working on it right now. Dear, can you take care of everything here?" Malcom asked Ester.

"I bet if you donate some money to the church, it might help," George suggested. "I think this will work, but you had better hurry, Malcom."

Malcom stood up. "I'm on my way. You best be ready when I return."

Cory and Etta looked at each other. Both of them were thinking that they must have missed something.

Ester stood. "Etta, I think it's time for us to freshen up. We will return in a few minutes."

Etta followed Ester upstairs.

When Etta and Ester returned, they were greeted by the men, Grandmother Beatrice, and Pastor Jones, waiting in the parlor. The atmosphere felt thick with anticipation, and Etta glanced at Cory, silently urging him to explain.

Cory stepped forward, taking Etta's hand gently in his. His eyes softened as he began to speak. "We've all discussed the situation and decided that the best course of action is to have a second wedding. Since we're not certain we can locate Miss Miller, and her signature is still missing from the marriage certificate, this ensures everything is legal and above board. By remarrying, I'll meet the special clause in the will, and Mr. Warren will have no grounds to challenge us. Not that I would ever let him take you away," he added, his voice firm. "But this guarantees you'll be legally, officially mine."

His lips curved into a warm smile, "And as a bonus, Grandmother will be able to attend the ceremony, along with Cousin Ester and Malcom."

Etta's heart swelled as Cory's words sank in. Relief washed over her, mingling with a joy, knowing their union would soon be indisputable. The weight of her earlier tension melted away, replaced by a sense of hope. A gentle smile spread across her face as she looked up at him, gratitude shining in her eyes. "I've prayed we'd find Miss Miller to sign the original certificate, but I like this solution much better. I'm so grateful to have your family here for this. It makes it more special."

She caught a glimpse of herself in a mirror across the room, relieved she had taken the time to leave her hair down and freshen up. She had no idea this morning that today would be her wedding day again. But as unexpected as it was, it felt right. It felt safe. Most importantly, she felt truly loved. The thought of having friends present at this wedding made it even more special, filling her heart with warmth and anticipation.

The atmosphere in the room was joyous. People may have thought she had lived in sin for the last few weeks, but that would soon be cleared up and in her heart they were already truly married.

Cory took her hand and handed her a single red rose. Etta looked into his green eyes and saw love shining in them.

"Ester explained all about Warner. You won't have to fear him anymore. I will protect you."

A tear rolled down Etta's face. "I'm sorry."

"There is no need to apologize. There are always men like that who are willing to use a bad situation to their advantage," Cory said. "Etta, will you do me the honor and marry me again?" Cory knew he wanted to spend the rest of his life with this woman. She rescued him and now he wanted to make sure she was rescued too.

"Yes," Etta replied

Taking a hankie out of his pocket, he gently wiped the tear from her face. He tucked her hand in his arm and led her to Pastor Jones.

"Are you ready?" he asked.

"I would like to open in prayer. Lord, we thank you for the hand you have had over this couple and that you will continue to have over them. Amen."

Sheriff John quietly entered the room and stood in the back. He didn't want to interrupt the ceremony.

Pastor Jones looked down at his Bible. "Dearly beloved, we are gathered together here in the sight of God, and in the face of this company of witnesses to join together this man and this woman in holy matrimony. The pastor's words seemed to fade for a minute while she looked into her husband's handsome eyes, but then she heard the words, love, honor, and obey until death. She pledged her whole heart to Cory.

"I now pronounce you husband and wife. You may kiss the bride."

Cory leaned in and kissed his beautiful wife. He wished they were alone as he heard his grandmother cough. He broke the kiss and kept his arm around her as his friends and family congratulated them.

"I would appreciate the witnesses signing the certificate. I will personally take the paper to the courthouse and make sure it is recorded," George said. Everyone waited as the paper was signed.

"Do we have all the signatures?" Cory asked.

George looked over the paper. "Yes, we do."

"What about Mr. Warner?" Etta asked worriedly.

"We are legally married. There is nothing he can do to you now and if he does our lawyers will handle it," Cory stated.

Sheriff John interrupted. "I have a message from Mr. Warner. He said that he will walk away from Etta if you pay him a thousand dollars."

Everyone gasped.

"What did you say to that, John?" Cory asked.

"I laughed at him and told him good luck with that," Sheriff John said.

Cory could feel his temper rise as he looked at George.

George nodded his head. "I will make inquires and see what I can do to get him removed from that banking business. Men like that are in the wrong business."

"I will also make some inquiries," Malcom echoed.

"Let's not mar this happy occasion with any more mention of that man. Did everyone sign the marriage certificate this time? Because I want to make sure my new granddaughter's last name is Vanderbilt. I enjoy having her around," Grandmother said with a smile. "Now, let's celebrate this marriage with some dessert and lemonade. There will be coffee for those that wish it."

After dessert, they retired back to the sitting room. But someone had moved the couches back and the rug had been removed. Grandmother put a record on the gramophone.

"May I have this dance, darling?" Cory asked Etta with his hand extended.

"I would love to. It has been ages since I danced," Etta said as his arms went around her. As they danced to the record, Etta felt like she was floating on a cloud. She prayed that Warren was in her past.

"Darling, I know you lost your house. Was there anything in it that you wanted? I can arrange to send for it," Cory offered.

"I sold everything that could bring in money. I have a couple little things still left from my parents that are worth more than money. But that is my past and you are my future."

Sheriff John came up to them once they sat down. "I'm glad that everything is now straightened out. I need to head home. I look forward to celebrating your marriage and welcoming Etta to our town on Sunday after church. If you need me, you know where I am."

"Thank you, John. Good night," Cory said.

George was the next to leave. "Now that everything is settled, at least for the moment, I am going to call it a night. Don't worry, I will look into it all and keep my eye on it."

"Thank you, George." Cory shook hands with him. "Good night and thank you."

"You're welcome and good night," George said before he left.

Ester and Malcom were next to leave and then Grandmother said, "It was a lovely wedding. I'm so glad I got to see it. Good night."

"I'm glad you could be part of it, Grandmother. Good night," Cory said as he kissed her cheek. She walked away.

"We are finally alone," Cory said softly before drawing her into a kiss.

Etta melted into his arms, her heart swelling with gratitude. She couldn't believe how blessed she was to have a mail-order husband who turned out to be so kind and gentle. She had been blessed to be rescued by a wonderful man. "Thank you, Lord," she whispered, her voice full of emotions.

"Yes, thank you, Lord," Cory echoed, his voice steady and heartfelt. He looked into her eyes, a smile spreading across his face. "And thank you for rescuing me, Etta. You've given me more than I ever hoped for."

As they stood there in the quiet, holding each other, the future stretched out before them. A future they would face together, hand in hand.

Paulette D. Marshall

The Railroad Tycoon Rescue

Epilogue

Sunday morning Cory was waiting for Etta and Grandmother in the entry way. The carriage was ready to take them to church. It was their one-year anniversary, and afterward he was taking his wife and grandmother to the Italian restaurant in town to celebrate. Even though Rosabella and Lucas owned the restaurant, they were going to join them, along with some other friends, to help celebrate their anniversary. Cory had reserved the whole restaurant so many of their friends could be with them.

Etta was looking forward to it even though she was moving slowly. Their first child was due any day now. Cory couldn't be more pleased about the upcoming event. His life had taken a change for the better. The railroad business was booming, but he also had learned to take time for family too. He realized that he had to balance it all and make sure that God was number one in their family.

Last year, once everything was straightened out surrounding the train accident, Cory had convinced Etta to take another train ride in a luxurious Pullman car for their honeymoon. It had taken some coaxing. Etta was understandably hesitant after the traumatic event, but Cory had assured her it would be different this time.

The investigation into the accident revealed that the tragedy was caused by someone using substandard metal, replacing the specified thickness with an inferior material. A man had pocketed the money that should have purchased the thicker metal. The railway company dismissed him from his position and worked quickly to repair the damage.

Cory had personally overseen the process, ensuring that everything was done correctly this time. He had paid the workers extra and authorized overtime to ensure the tracks were replaced as quickly and safely as possible. Within two weeks, the line was operational again with everyone's hard work and dedication.

When Etta finally stepped aboard the Pullman car for their honeymoon, the luxury and comfort of the ride seemed to melt away some of her lingering fears. She had relaxed leaning against Cory as they watched the scenery glide by. She managed to put some of her fears aside on that trip.

The trip would be one that she would treasure for years to come.

Cory vowed to himself that he would make sure to take time with her every year for a vacation for just the two of them together. He wanted to make sure that he could give her an extra special trip since she was always giving so freely to others. She was constantly making sure that he had everything that he needed. How had he gotten so lucky?

One day, Cory admitted to her that he felt bad about not originally sending the Pullman car for her. "I'm sorry I couldn't send a Pullman car to get you, but that would have revealed that I had money. I realize now that not everyone is only interested in money. I am one lucky man."

Etta kissed his cheek and said, "I understand, dear. I love you for who you are and not your money. If we should lose all your money tomorrow, I will still love you."

Cory smiled and replied with a kiss to her lips.

Etta hated to ask, but she really wanted to know, "What did happen with Warren?" She had wanted to ask many times, but she had been afraid.

"Well, my dear, he is spending time in jail now. He was found guilty of embezzling, and they are still trying to prove he murdered his first wife," Cory had admitted. "As for that loan that was supposed to be against your house, that was fabricated. You still own your house, and I have made sure it was fixed up to its glory days. It is my gift to you. You may sell it or keep it. It's whatever you want, darling."

Etta was surprised. "I still own the house? Do you think that we can take a vacation there sometime so that I may visit with my dear friend?"

"That sounds like a good idea," Cory agreed.

"I might just give it to Mabel and Mack. Their home is small. I will have to pray about it," Etta said. Realizing that Warren hadn't taken her house made her heart lighter. She didn't need the house anymore since she had her home with Cory. Mable and Mack would take good care of it for her, and she couldn't wait to visit them.

"I think that is a good idea." Cory said with a smile. He was glad that his gift had made her happy. "Sweetheart, I want to thank you for rescuing me. Without you, I might have lost the railroad, but more importantly I might have missed out on all of this and your love."

"I want to thank you for rescuing me. I don't think I could have lasted much longer," Etta replied, her voice filled with emotion. "I think we are both blessed, and I thank the Lord for bringing us together and rescuing both of us. I love you with all of my heart."

"And I love you with all of my heart too, sweetheart," Cory had replied, his voice warm and filled with sincerity. He hadn't realized just how much he needed rescuing until Etta came into his life. Nor had he imagined how deeply he could love someone.

Etta had transformed his world in ways he never thought possible. She brought light, laughter, and a sense of purpose that had been missing. Together, they had created something beautiful, something he couldn't imagine living without. She wasn't just his wife; she was his heart and his home.

Who would have guessed that they both needed rescuing? Perhaps that was exactly how the Lord had planned it all along.

The End

Paulette D. Marshall

The Railroad Tycoon Rescue

Bible Verse

We know that in all things God works for the good of those who love him, who have been called according to his purpose.

Romans 8:28

Paulette D. Marshall

Vanilla Cake

1 cup unsalted butter, softened.

1 ½ cup granulated sugar

4 large eggs, room temperature

1 tablespoon vanilla extract

2 ¾ cups cake flour

2 ¾ teaspoon baking powder

½ teaspoon salt

1 cup whole milk, room temperature

Instructions:

1. Preheat the oven to 350. Lightly grease the sides and bottom of 2 9 inches round cake pans. Line the bottom with parchment paper cut to fit and generously grease the parchment paper as well. Dust the pans with flour then tap out any excess; set aside.
2. In a large bowl, beat the butter and sugar together until light and fluffy, about 5 minutes. Add the eggs, one at a time, mixing well after each addition. Beat in the vanilla.
3. Combine the flour, baking powder, and salt in a medium bowl. Stir with a whisk and add it to the butter mixture followed by the milk. Beat at medium-low speed just until combined.
4. Divide the batter evenly between the prepared pans. Bake for 20 -30 minutes or until a toothpick inserted into the center comes out with a few moist crumbs attached. Take care not to over-bake. Check the cake at 15

The Railroad Tycoon Rescue
minutes to see how it is doing and judge the timing from there.
5. Cool for 10 minutes. Remove from pans and cool completely on a wire rack.

Paulette D. Marshall

The Railroad Tycoon Rescue

About the author: Paulette D. Marshall

Paulette loves writing sweet, clean, wholesome, inspirational romantic stories with a powerful sense of family, community, and usually a happy ending. She writes in Christian genres: historical, time travel romance, contemporary, romance, small town romance, western, and sometime adds a little mystery thrown in too. Who knows what she is going to write next?

She and her husband live in a small town in Northern California along with her three miniature Shih Tzu dogs. They are blessed with four beautiful children, one wonderful son-in-law and five beautiful grandchildren. Some of her favorite things are spending time in her garden during spring, summer, and fall while enjoying her beautiful flowers. She especially enjoys watching the butterflies and bees. She loves watching quail come into their yard or see an eagle soar by and watching the snow fall in the winter, while sitting by the fire. She loves to do crafts, cook, and sew, along with writing, or snuggle with her dogs.

Paulette is also an avid reader when she is not writing her books. She has always wanted to write and due to health issues, she can now. She also enjoys doing research. When traveling, she and her husband love to visit historical sites.

Paulette D. Marshall

Historical Note

One of Nevada's oldest settlements started when two miners, Pat McLaughlin and Peter O'Reilly discovered gold at the head of Six-Mile Canyon in 1859. Soon, another miner, Henry Comstock, stumbled upon their find and claimed it was on his property. The gullible McLaughlin and O'Reilly believed him, which assured Henry a place in history when the giant Comstock Lode was named.

However, the Comstock Lode would not be known for gold but rather for its immensely rich silver deposits. Though silver was initially discovered in 1857 in Nevada by brothers Ethan and Hosea Grosh, they died before recording their claims. Though the miners rushed in after discovering gold, they could not get to it because of the heavy blue-gray clay that clung to picks and shovel. However, when someone had the good sense to assay the sticky mud, it was found to be worth $2,000 a ton.

Within no time, a ramshackle town of tens and shacks was born. When a miner named James Finney, who was mor often call "Old Virginny" from his birthplace, dropped a bottle of whiskey on the ground, he christened the newly founded ten and dugout town "Old Virginny Town" in honor of himself. It was later changed to Virginia City.

The Railroad Tycoon Rescue
Want to know more about the people in Virgina City?

You can find them in Rosabella's Dream and Ester's Dreams stories.

Both stories are combined in Dreams of Love book.

7